The Hidden Man

MURDER ON TRIAL
MURDER MADE ABSOLUTE
DEATH ON REMAND
FALSE WITNESS
LAWFUL PURSUIT
ARM OF THE LAW
CAUSE OF DEATH
DEATH BY MISADVENTURE
ADAM'S CASE
THE CASE AGAINST PHILIP QUEST
GIRL FOUND DEAD
THE CRIME OF COLIN WISE
THE UNPROFESSIONAL SPY
THE ANXIOUS CONSPIRATOR
A CRIME APART
THE MAN WHO DIED ON FRIDAY
THE MAN WHO KILLED TOO SOON
THE SHADOW GAME
THE SILENT LIARS
SHEM'S DEMISE
A TROUT IN THE MILK
REWARD FOR A DEFECTOR
A PINCH OF SNUFF
THE JUROR
MENACES, MENACES
MURDER WITH MALICE
THE FATAL TRIP
CROOKED WOOD
ANYTHING BUT THE TRUTH
SMOOTH JUSTICE
VICTIM OF CIRCUMSTANCE
A CLEAR CASE OF SUICIDE
CRIME UPON CRIME
DOUBLE JEOPARDY
HAND OF FATE
GODDESS OF DEATH
A PARTY TO MURDER
DEATH IN CAMERA

Michael Underwood The Hidden Man

St. Martin's Press
New York

Library of Congress Cataloging in Publication Data

Underwood, Michael, 1916-
  The hidden man.

  I. Title.
PR6055.V3H5   1985   823'.914   84-22302
ISBN 0-312-37196-9

First published in Great Britain by Macmillan London Ltd.

First U.S. Edition

10 9 8 7 6 5 4 3 2 1

For Mark Hamilton

The Hidden Man

Prologue

JONATHAN COOL TO STAR IN NEW T.V. SERIES
JONATHAN COOL IN MILLION DOLLAR T.V. DEAL
BRITAIN'S MUMS HOT ON COOL

These and similar headlines appeared in the popular press during the last weeks of October, proving once more that Jonathan Cool was big news, as, indeed, he had been for the past twelve months.

He might not be the first lead singer of a pop group to turn serious actor, but no other had succeeded in projecting an image that had such an appeal for the nation at large. Girls mobbed him whenever they had the opportunity and their mothers had recently voted him a favourite son, or an even more favourite son-in-law. At twenty-four he neither smoked nor drank and his photograph radiated a fresh and youthful friendliness. The sceptics averred that nobody could possess so many virtues without being an insufferable prig and yet those who knew him said it wasn't so. He was, they insisted, a genuinely wholesome and charming young man, his head unturned by all the adulation and by a bank account that visibly swelled even while his bank manager warmed his hands over it.

Naturally enough his private life constantly came under a microscope, but he managed to conduct it with extreme discretion, and the fact remained that none of the girls with whom his name had ever been linked had yet been lured into telling a story that would have boosted a newspaper's sales by a single copy.

For the past twelve months he had been riding the crest of a cream-topped wave and, with a business manager as determined and astute as Paula Lang, seemed destined to remain there, if not indefinitely, at least for the foreseeable future.

It was Paula who had insisted he should change his name. The family name was Coolie, which, she said briskly, conjured up a picture of peasants in lampshade hats. He could never become a star with a name like that. Thus he had shaved off the final two letters and become Cool.

It had also been Paula who had persuaded a popular newspaper to organise the poll which had resulted in the headline that 'Britain's mums were hot on Cool'. A considerable percentage of the over-forties polled had, in fact, said that they wouldn't mind swapping their own husbands for him, but the paper concerned ('ours is a family readership') had thought it wiser to omit this tantalising statistic.

It was shortly after these headlines had appeared in the press that Jonathan drove down to Worthing in his Lotus to see his current girlfriend, Cheryl Peterson. Cheryl was eighteen, an only child and completely infatuated with him. She had now known him for three months, having first met him at a party in London to which she had been invited by her cousin who was a production secretary on the television series Jonathan was then making.

The point had been reached when her mother, Joan, and her father, Stan, who was a clerk in a local solicitor's office, felt they could even hear distant wedding bells, with all the dreamlike prospect of reflected fame and fortune that implied.

'Cheryl home yet?' Stan called out as he arrived home shortly after half-past five that Friday evening.

'She's upstairs getting ready,' his wife replied from the kitchen.

'What time's Jonathan coming?'

'He's picking her up at seven.'

'She'll bring him in for a drink of course.'

'I don't know what their plans are.'

Stan frowned. 'I'll tell her to,' he said firmly. 'Can't have him driving all this way and not coming in.'

'Don't make a thing of it, Stan! If he doesn't want to come in, don't make a fuss. I have the feeling that our Cheryl's a bit on edge.'

'You think he may be going to propose to her this evening?' he asked with sudden eagerness.

'I've no idea.'

'He ought to speak to me first. After all I am her father and there is a proper way of doing these things, even in this day and age.' *Even in this day and age* was one of his favourite expressions.

Though his wife was just as excited as he was at the possibility of Cheryl becoming Mrs Cool, she was more restrained in voicing her hopes and feelings. Cheryl herself said little (she had never confided much in her parents), but with Jonathan calling her on the phone every day and making frequent visits to Worthing, she couldn't fail to have her hopes about marriage.

Occasionally she had visited him at his flat off Baker Street, but on the whole he preferred to meet her on neutral ground as reporters were liable to hang around the block where he lived and pounce on his visitors. Soon, he told Cheryl, he would be buying a place with greater privacy and things would be different. What had most impressed her about his present flat, she had told her mother, had been its extreme tidiness. The coffee jar always had its lid on, and the various tubes and bottles in the bathroom stood in perfect array. These two details had particularly impressed her.

On the occasions he came down to Worthing they would invariably go to a club at nearby Goring which was run by an ex-member of his old group. Here he was guaranteed discretion, which almost amounted to anonymity. Moreover, Micky, the owner, would make a room upstairs available, so that he and Cheryl could be together without fear of interruption or intrusion.

'You're looking as pretty as a picture,' Joan Peterson said when her daughter appeared in the kitchen doorway. 'Is that the dress Jonathan gave you?' she asked, knowing perfectly well that it was.

'It must have cost him a few quid,' her father remarked, coming up behind. 'Got one of those fancy French labels, has it?'

'Dior,' Cheryl said.

'It's really lovely,' her mother purred.

'And the perfume,' her father said with a noisy sniff, 'is that

French too?'

'Chanel.'

'One of the best,' he said with an approving nod. Turning to his wife, he went on, 'Tell you what, why don't we get Jonathan down for Sunday dinner next weekend? What do you say Cheryl?'

'He'll be away,' she said in a subdued voice.

'Away? Where's he going?' her father enquired with the note of belligerence that was never far below the surface.

'He's flying to Hollywood next Wednesday to discuss a film.'

'How long for?'

'About a week. He's stopping off in New York on his way back.'

'Calling you every day from there'll put his phone bill up,' Stan said heartily. Then, giving his wife a meaningful glance, he added, 'He ought to take you along too.'

'Don't be silly, dad!'

'I don't know what's silly about it.'

'I know what you and mum are thinking, but give it a rest.'

'Give what a rest?' her father said indignantly.

'You know what I mean. Don't try and rush us. Maybe. . .' She bit the sentence off as though wishing she had never begun it.

'Maybe what?' her father asked eagerly.

She gave an impatient shrug, leaving her parents to pursue their own thoughts.

It was about an hour later when they were in the front room with the television on that they heard a car pull up outside. Stan immediately sprang to his feet, followed by his daughter.

'It's O.K., dad,' she said, 'we're going straight off.'

'Aren't you going to ask him in?' he enquired militantly.

'We'll be late,' Cheryl said breathlessly. 'Don't wait up for me, I'll see you in the morning.'

'Late for what?' her father demanded as she pushed past him into the hall.

But she had had enough of this delaying dialogue, and made a dash for the front door.

'Night, mum! Night, dad,' she called out as she slammed it behind her.

'What's she up to?' Stan grumbled as he returned to the living-room. 'Is she suddenly ashamed of us, not asking him in?'

'Of course she isn't.'

'Well, why didn't she ask him in then? We've always treated him as one of the family.'

'Come and sit down and stop fussing.'

'I just hope he'll remember that he needs my permission to marry our Cheryl,' he said huffily. 'There are certain proprieties to be observed even in this day and age.'

His wife said nothing. Frankly she couldn't care less whether the so-called proprieties were observed or not. She would even forgo the glamour of a slap-up wedding provided Jonathan became her son-in-law. Her feminine instinct told her that tonight was the night he was going to pop the question. She felt he would wish to have it settled before he went off to America and she wondered how soon it would be before the nation was made aware that Jonathan Cool had chosen a bride. She realised that she must be prepared for a tumultuous invasion of their privacy which would inevitably follow the announcement. She imagined it would be similar to what Princess Di had gone through before *her* marriage.

In the event, however, it was not Jonathan Cool's forthcoming wedding that made the news the next day, but his violent death the previous evening.

Chapter 1

'Mr Jameson's', as it was popularly known, (or Mr Jameson's School of the English Language, to grace it with its full name) had recently celebrated its fiftieth anniversary and was regarded as one of the town's institutions. Its founder and sole proprietor, Horace Chadwick Jameson, was still going strong at eighty and was still the school's vital force.

During the whole of its existence it had been situated in a double-fronted early Victorian villa in Swift Road, which lay about half a mile back from Worthing's sea front in a residential area.

Mr Jameson was a character with a large C. He was tall and thin and had a mane of white hair and a walrus moustache. His complexion was pickled brown, which accentuated the blueness of his eyes. When on duty he always dressed the same, black jacket and waistcoat and a pair of striped trousers. He possessed several such outfits and all were now of equal shabbiness. He wore a stiff winged collar and a black tie which provided the background for a large pearl pin. On his feet were old-fashioned black boots with thick crêpe soles. Almost as old as himself was the bicycle which he would ride down to the sea front most days for an early morning dip.

His students were all foreigners, mostly in their twenties, and the courses they attended were of varying duration. Ornately inscribed diplomas were awarded to those who passed their final exams. Those who failed went away with a mere certificate of attendance signed by the school secretary, whereas all diplomas bore Mr Jameson's own elaborate signature.

Apart from Mr Jameson, the teaching staff consisted of Peter

Atkins, Cecily Young and Eileen Tiplady. Miss Young and Miss Tiplady were ladies in their fifties who lived with widowed mothers. Peter Atkins was only in his mid-forties and had been on the staff less time than the others. He had, however, married Mr Jameson's secretary, Sarah, and they had a daughter, Nicole, aged two, who was the joy of their life. Sarah, who was twelve years younger than her husband, still worked part-time at the school and did a lot of the secretarial work from home.

Mr Jameson's zest for living was demonstrated by the number of parties he gave. There was a party at the beginning of every term and another at the end; there were parties at Christmas and Easter, mid-summer parties and, of course, a party on his birthday, which fell at the end of October.

The composition of each party was virtually the same, only the students supplying fresh faces. Usually three or four (six at the most) would be asked, selected by Mr Jameson for their passable English and presentable manners. The guests were otherwise made up of staff and a hard core of locals. Mr and Mrs Morgan who ran a small hotel in the same road always attended, as did Major Bloomfield, their oldest permanent resident, who was the same age as Mr Jameson. Mr and Mrs Gatling, who lived opposite the school, never missed; nor did old Mrs Christian, a wealthy widow with a living-in staff.

Conviviality was the keynote of all Mr Jameson's parties. Everyone contributed his quota of life and soul to the proceedings, fortified by Mr Jameson's home-brewed punch. Served hot in winter and ice-cold in summer, its recipe was Mr Jameson's own closely guarded secret, chiefly because he never clearly remembered from one occasion to the next exactly what he put into it. The basis was cheap red wine, thereafter its preparation was something like a mystery tour.

'I'll be along about five o'clock,' Sarah said to her husband as he prepared to leave the house and catch a bus to work that morning. She let out a sigh. 'I still haven't got Jamie a birthday present. I'll have to think of something.'

'A new pair of bicycle-clips, perhaps,' her husband remarked gravely.

13

Sarah laughed. 'It's an idea. I mean, I might get him something for his bicycle.'

Peter shook his head in a bemused fashion. Surely she had realised his suggestion was intended as a joke.

'Don't look so solemn, darling!' Sarah said, giving him a parting kiss.

'I hope you and Nicole have a happy day,' he said in the tone that always melted her.

Sarah returned to the breakfast alcove to find Nicole gazing out of the window with a faraway look. There were times when her expressions mirrored those of her father so uncannily that Sarah would find herself holding her breath for fear of breaking a spell. Although Nicole could be as lively and talkative as most two-year-olds, she could also assume the same thoughtfully grave air that was so much Peter's.

As she stood quietly observing her daughter, her mind went back three-and-a-half years to the day when Peter had arrived at the school for interview. She remembered showing him into Mr Jameson's study and crossing her fingers that he would make a good impression. She felt he was just what the school needed, though a deeper analysis of her feelings might have disclosed a more personal motive.

'I think I'll give Mr Atkins a try,' Mr Jameson had said to her afterwards.

'You liked him then?' Sarah had said a trifle breathlessly.

Mr Jameson had shot her a faintly quizzical look before replying, 'I liked the clarity of his diction.'

Three months after Peter joined the staff, he and Sarah became engaged. Three months later they were married, an occasion which provided an admirable excuse for an additional Mr Jameson party. Nicole was born on the first anniversary of their wedding day.

Nicole suddenly turned her head and gave her mother a ravishing smile.

'Potty,' she said, bringing Sarah back from her bout of nostalgia.

Later in the morning they went out and Sarah bought Mr

14

Jameson a silver paper-knife from the funny little shop that was the source of many of her presents. It would look elegant on his desk, even if he never used it. Certainly more expensive, though probably less practical than a pair of bicycle clips, she reflected on their way home.

At half-past four the baby-sitter arrived and fifteen minutes later Sarah set off in the car, with the paper-knife gift-wrapped on the seat beside her.

'We'll be back by half ten, Rosemary,' she said as she prepared to leave. 'The party won't last that long, but I have to help with the clearing up.'

'Don't worry about me, I'll be all right,' Rosemary said reassuringly, holding Nicole in her arms.

She was the seventeen-year-old daughter of a neighbour, who was their regular baby-sitter. Nicole adored her and once she had been put to bed, Rosemary would settle down to her A-level studies. She always came armed with a pile of books.

Though the party was not scheduled to start till six, Sarah knew she would be expected to add any finishing touches to the preparations before the guests arrived. Mr Jameson would have shut himself away in the pantry and would be concocting his punch with all the absorption of an ancient alchemist.

The guests would arrive more or less together on the stroke of six and would stay until the end at half-past eight when they would sally forth en masse. It was a familiar and accepted pattern. On this particular occasion everyone would bring Mr Jameson a birthday present which he would open with great ceremony and relish while his guests watched and offered suitably appraising comments.

It was halfway through the party that Sarah glanced across the room to where her husband was deep in conversation with old Mrs Christian. At least, he was standing with a grave, attentive expression while she did the talking.

She'd carry him off to her lair if she could, Sarah reflected with faint amusement and a sudden unexpected twinge of jealousy. She's boring Peter to tears and he'll drink more than he should. Then she gave a small shrug. What did it matter! She would do

15

the driving home anyway. Nevertheless she didn't like him drinking too much on these occasions, even if the only visible effect was a certain moroseness.

'A splendid party, I thought,' Mr Jameson said contentedly as he waved the last guest into the night.

'All your parties are,' Sarah observed loyally.

'Where's your husband got to?' he enquired, looking around.

'I've put him to work in the kitchen.'

'Good chap! Will it take long to clear up?' He had a way of putting the question with childlike innocence.

'No. Why don't you go and sit down and we'll soon have everything straight.'

'If you're sure I can't help. . .' he murmured as he ambled off in the direction of his study. 'Come and say good night before you go. Don't be afraid to wake me up if I happen to have dropped off,' he added with a yawn.

An hour later when they were ready to leave, Sarah opened the study door and peered in.

'He looks as peaceful as Nicole when she's asleep,' she whispered to Peter. In a slightly raised voice she said, 'We're going, Jamie.'

'Drive carefully, my dear,' he said in a fuzzy tone without opening his eyes. 'I'm not really asleep. Just resting my eyes.'

'Thank goodness we haven't far to drive,' Sarah remarked as she took Peter's arm on the pavement outside. 'The car's just round the corner.'

A sea mist had blown in and everywhere was unnaturally silent.

'We'll soon be home,' Sarah said reassuringly as they reached the car. Peter was inclined to be a nervous passenger in any weather that was less than perfect and she could feel his tension. 'I've driven in much worse than this and I know the way backwards.'

The mist proved to be variable with visibilty up to a hundred yards and more in some places, but much less in others.

It was just after they had entered one particularly dense patch that it all happened.

16

Peter suddenly let out an inarticulate shout at the same moment as there was a chilling thud and a sound of heavy scraping. Sarah braked immediately and gave her husband a horrified glance.

'I think you have knocked somebody down,' he said in an expressionless voice.

'Oh, my God! Let's pray they're not badly hurt,' Sarah exclaimed in anguish.

As if to answer her invocation, a girl's face rose up like an apparition in front of the windscreen.

'You've killed him,' she screamed. 'You've killed him!'

Chapter 2

Sarah thought the screams would never cease. They did, of course, but only to be repeated every time somebody fresh appeared on the scene. The noise had brought people out from their houses and they drifted before Sarah's eyes like wraiths in the heavy mist. She sat in the driver's seat too shocked to move. Peter had meanwhile got out and was bending over the body in the road.

'She killed him,' the girl screamed more hysterically than ever when a police car containing three uniformed officers arrived. Sarah could see the girl's accusing finger and shrank back in her seat as though it were a branding iron.

Eventually the girl was led away to one of the houses and Sarah saw Peter speaking to one of the officers who approached her window. She wound it down.

'It might be best if you come and sit in our car for a while,' he said in a not unfriendly tone. 'You're not injured, are you?' Sarah shook her head and he went on, 'It'll be easier to deal with the formalities there.'

He helped her out and guided her by the arm to where the police car was parked. She got into the back and he walked round and got in beside her.

'I'm Sergeant Hibbert. What's your name?'

'Atkins. Sarah Atkins.'

'Mrs Atkins, is it?'

'Yes. That was my husband you were speaking to just now.'

'Where do you live, Mrs Atkins?'

She gave him their address and added in a whisper, 'We were on our way home when this happened.'

'Where had you been spending the evening?'

'At Mr Jameson's in Swift Road. It's a language school. My husband teaches there.'

'Yes, I know Mr Jameson's by name.' He peered at her more closely. 'Have you been drinking at all this evening, Mrs Atkins?'

'I had a glass or two of punch,' she said with a sudden feeling of utter despair. 'It was Mr Jameson's birthday,' she added, as though this might somehow make it all right.

'I'm afraid I shall have to ask you to take a breath test. It's become a formality these days in traffic cases. We can do it in the car. It won't take a moment.'

'I'd like my husband to be present,' Sarah said in the tone of one expressing a dying wish.

Sergeant Hibbert glanced out of the window. 'He seems to have disappeared,' he remarked. 'He's probably not far away, but there's nothing he can do to help, so why don't we get it over with? I ought to tell you, Mrs Atkins, that it's an offence to refuse to take the test, other than on special medical grounds.'

He instructed her what to do before handing her the tube into which to blow.

'Hmm!' he observed judicially as he examined the result. 'It seems you're over the legal limit, Mrs Atkins. In these circumstances I'm afraid I have to arrest you, but don't be alarmed. There'll be a further breath test at the police station and if it's still positive, we'll require a blood or urine sample.' Noticing Sarah's look of blank horror, he said, not unsympathetically, 'Probably the punch was a bit stronger than you thought it was. Those sort of mixtures can be pretty deadly.' After a slight pause he went on, 'When we get to the station you'll also be able to make a statement saying exactly what happened.'

'I won't go without my husband,' she said with a note of suppressed hysteria.

'Of course, he can come along. He'll also be able to give us an account of what happened.'

'I must phone home and tell our baby-sitter that. . . that we shall be late.'

'That can easily be arranged. Here's your husband now.' He

wound down his window. 'Mr Atkins, we're about to take your wife to the police station to complete various formalities and I expect you'd like to accompany her.'

While she had been sitting in the police car, Sarah had been aware of two other police cars arriving, as well as an ambulance, which had quickly departed carrying with it her hopes and prayers for the injured occupant. Just because that girl had screamed at her didn't mean the person she had knocked down was dead. The girl was obviously hysterical and wouldn't have known for sure. He might be only unconscious and his injuries relatively superficial, but with a lot of blood spilled. People had survived far worse accidents than this one. It didn't need a miracle for him to be alive.

Sergeant Hibbert, who had left the car, now returned.

'I'm afraid I have bad news, Mrs Atkins,' he said. 'I've just heard that the person you knocked down died on the way to hospital. I understand his name was Jonathan Cool.'

'Not the actor?' Sarah said in a tone of further horror.

'I gather so. I suggest we go to the station right away.'

'What about our car?' Peter asked anxiously.

'I'll get an officer to drive it. As you'll appreciate, we shall need to examine it.'

Though Sergeant Hibbert was politeness itself, Sarah felt daunted by his air of firm authority.

'How long shall we be kept at the station?' she said when they were on their way.

'Not too long, I hope, Mrs Atkins.'

'And what'll happen after that?'

'We'll see that you get safely home.'

'What I mean is, will there be a court case?'

'All I can tell you, Mrs Atkins, is that we shall be submitting a report to headquarters and it'll be up to others to reach a decision. In view of the sort of public interest the matter is likely to arouse it could be referred to the Director of Public Prosecutions.'

Soon after arrival at the police station a doctor took a sample of Sarah's blood, a uniformed inspector having told her it was an

20

offence to refuse. Not that she would have anyway. All she wanted was to get home and see Nicole – and that as quickly as possible.

She had not been long at the station before becoming aware of intense activity all around her. Phones that had been silent began ringing incessantly and figures hurried to and fro along the corridor outside.

Sarah had been sitting alone in her misery in a small room when Sergeant Hibbert suddenly appeared. He was accompanied by a young woman whom he introduced as Woman Police Constable Illingworth.

'All hell's breaking loose,' he said with a sigh. 'The press have got on to the victim's identity. It was bound to happen sooner rather than later. Anyway, Mrs Atkins, if you care to make a statement and tell us exactly what happened, Miss Illingworth will write it down. Afterwards you can read it through, make any corrections you wish and sign it.'

'Oughtn't I to have a solicitor?'

'There'll be time enough for that later if you're going to be prosecuted. As I've explained, that's not going to be decided tonight. Just because somebody's been knocked down and killed doesn't make a prosecution inevitable. It depends on the evidence. Your evidence as much as anyone's.'

'But I've been breathalysed.'

'What happens about that depends on the analysis of the blood sample. Incidentally, you have been given part of the sample, haven't you?'

Sarah nodded and glanced with a shudder at her handbag in which she had put the small bottle containing her blood.

'All right then, Mrs Atkins, would you like to begin – at the beginning?'

'It was Mr Jameson's birthday, his eightieth as a matter of fact, and he had a party to celebrate. All the guests had departed by just half-past eight and my husband and I stayed on to clear up so that it was around ten o'clock before we were ready to leave. It was misty when we came out of the house. . .'

'How much did you have to drink in the course of the evening,

21

Mrs Atkins?' Sergeant Hibbert interrupted.

'About two glasses of punch.'

'*About* two. Might it have been three, or even four?'

'Definitely not as many as four.'

'Were glasses being topped up before they were actually empty? It happens at most parties.'

'Yes.'

'So that you may have drunk rather more than you intended?'

Sarah shook her head vigorously. 'I was very careful as I knew I was going to be driving home. I'm sure I didn't have more than a total of, say, two-and-a-half glasses.'

'What size glasses were they?'

'Wine glasses.'

'Big ones or small ones?'

'Medium.'

'And did you go on drinking while you were clearing up afterwards?'

'No. As a matter of fact I made myself a cup of coffee.'

'Was that because you. . .'

'No, it wasn't because I was worried about my condition,' Sarah broke in vehemently.

'So around ten o'clock you emerged into the cold night air to drive home?'

'Yes.'

'Did you feel all right?'

'Perfectly all right. I wouldn't have driven otherwise. Moreover, my husband wouldn't have let me drive if he hadn't thought I was fit to do so. We'd gone at least a mile-and-a-half before the accident happened. A mile-and-a-half of twists and turns and several sets of traffic lights. The mist was the only hazard, particularly as it was so patchy. As you know it was much thicker where the accident took place than a hundred yards further back.'

'Would you care to estimate your speed at the moment of impact?' Sergeant Hibbert asked.

'I've really no idea. Definitely not fast. It's not fair to press me on that.'

22

'Nobody's pressing you, Mrs Atkins.'

'All I can say is that I wasn't going any faster than was safe.'

'Can you explain why you didn't see Mr Cool?'

Sarah shook her head helplessly. 'I'd like to know what he was doing in the middle of the road in a fog. Didn't he realise the danger?'

'I understand he was about to get back into his car.'

'Where was his car?' Sarah asked with a frown.

'Parked at the side of the road.'

'I never saw any car. If it was there it definitely didn't have any lights on.'

Sergeant Hibbert gave her a sceptical look. 'Its yellow hazard lights were flashing and it was also showing the normal red tail lights.'

'It can't have,' Sarah cried out. 'I'd have seen them. . . they must have been switched on afterwards.'

'Do you want that put into your statement? That the lights must have been turned on after the accident?'

'Yes, because it's the truth. Ask my husband, he'll confirm what I've said.'

'Very likely,' he remarked in a tone that seemed to imply that he was used to husbands and wives backing up one another's lies. 'Anyway, you're maintaining that you never saw Mr Cool's car parked at the side of the road?'

'Because it wasn't displaying any lights despite the fog.'

'Do you think you'd have seen it if its rear lights had been showing? Not to mention its hazard lights!'

Although Sarah realised this was something of a trap question, she felt she had to answer it.

'I'm certain I would have done,' she said stoutly. 'But they weren't showing. The girl must have switched them on afterwards. The girl who did all the screaming.'

'Do you know anything about her, Mrs Atkins?'

'Nothing. I just assume she was in the car with him. His girlfriend, I imagine.'

Sergeant Hibbert nodded. 'Her name's Cheryl Peterson. She lives not far from where the accident took place. I understand she and Jonathan Cool had been out together and that he was taking her home before driving back to London.'

'Then what were they doing parked at the roadside without any lights?' Sarah said with a quiet note of triumph.

Sergeant Hibbert declined, however, to venture an answer and merely asked her whether there was anything further she wished to add to her statement.

'It's your statement, Mrs Atkins,' he said smoothly, adding somewhat tendentiously, 'You'll realise that I've only asked you questions in order to clear up possible ambiguities.'

'I can only repeat that I wasn't driving at all fast and that this person suddenly appeared from nowhere in front of the car.'

'Are you now saying that you did actually see him before the impact?'

'No, I'm not. I never saw him at all. There was just this horrible thud. You see, I was driving by the cat's eyes in the centre of the road, so that my attention was more on my offside than my nearside.' She paused. 'But please put in that I'm absolutely positive his car wasn't showing any lights at the time of the accident.'

Half an hour later, still shocked and stunned by what had happened, she and Peter sat in silence in the back of the police car driving them home. Peter held her hand in his and from time to time gave it a fond squeeze.

It was only after the baby-sitter had departed and they were alone together that she flung herself into his arms and clung desperately to him.

'Tell me everything's going to be all right,' she said in a choked voice.

'Of course it will be, my darling,' he replied, hugging her tightly.

'And if I do have to go to court, you'll stand by me?' Thrusting her head back and staring straight up into his face she went on in an urgent tone, 'It's true, isn't it, that the other car didn't have any lights on?'

He nodded. 'I told the police that.'

She let out a slow sigh. 'I'm frightened, Peter, but I'd be even more so if I didn't have you to give me strength.' After a slight pause she added, 'A court has got to believe us.'

He pressed her head against his shoulder and kissed her lightly on the forehead.

'We'd better go and make sure Nicole's all right,' he said steering her towards the door. 'We won't talk any more about what's happened until tomorrow. We're both exhausted.'

At Peter's insistence she took one of his sleeping pills and quickly fell into a dreamless sleep.

The nightmares were to come later.

Chapter 3

During the next few days Sarah kept to the house as much as possible. When obliged to go out she had the horrible feeling that people were staring at her and whispering behind her back.

The popular press had had, and were still having, a field day over Jonathan Cool's death. Every detail of his short life was duly embellished and fed to an apparently avid public. There might be natural and man-made disasters taking place around the world, but all made way for news of Jonathan Cool's demise. An earthquake in Turkey killing twelve hundred people in a landslide of rubble and mud made nothing like the same impact as Cool's death on a late October evening in a staid seaside town.

Cheryl Peterson had overcome her grief sufficiently to talk to reporters. She spoke at length of her and Jonathan's love for one another and said that she was determined to dedicate the rest of her life to his memory. Nobody pressed her to explain exactly what that would involve. When asked about the accident, she didn't hesitate to throw all the blame on the driver of the offending car. Her father, too, had chimed in, vehemently demanding that justice should be done, adding that there were far too many reckless drivers around.

Feeling herself surrounded by hostility, Sarah was thankful that Cool's funeral was to be held in faraway Norfolk where his parents lived. She couldn't have borne it taking place on her own doorstep.

'I still can't believe it's really happened,' she said to Mr Jameson a few days later.

It was the first time she had been to the school since the evening of the party. They were sitting in his study and he was gazing at her thoughtfully across his desk, rather like a shrewd but benign old bird of the forest.

'It'll blow over sooner than you expect,' he said. 'All this newspaper rubbish, I mean. They live from one seven-day wonder to the next and on the eighth day they find some fresh drama to write about.'

'It'll start up all over again if I have to go to court,' Sarah said wearily.

'I'm afraid that's probably true. Incidentally, have you been to a solicitor yet?' ·

'There doesn't seem any point until I know definitely that I'm being charged. To go and see one now would, I feel, somehow invite a prosecution. I know that's silly, but I don't want to have to think about it unless I'm obliged to.' She paused. 'Anyway I don't fancy going to a local one.'

'I understand that, so may I suggest one I know in London?'

Sarah looked at him in surprise. 'You think I ought to consult one straightaway, Jamie?'

He nodded. 'Yes, I do. After all there's bound to be an inquest, whether or not you're proceeded against and you'll want to have your interests looked after.'

'Who do you suggest?' she asked with a note of reluctance.

'Rosa Epton. She's a partner in a firm called Snaith and Epton which specialises in criminal cases.'

Sarah frowned. 'I don't ever recall having heard you mention her name. I thought you always dealt with Mr Henshaw in the town.'

'Rosa's the daughter of an old friend of mine who died a few years ago. He was the rector of a village in Herefordshire. I'd not seen her since she was a schoolgirl until last month. You remember I went up to London to attend a meeting at the Department of Education – and a fine waste of time that proved to be – well, afterwards I went along to that exhibition of school equipment at Olympia, which was another waste of time. Anyway, when I came out I was looking for a café where I could sit down and have a cup of tea when I bumped into Rosa. I doubt whether I'd have recognised her, but she came up and greeted me

27

by name.' He paused. 'Didn't I tell you all this when I got back?'

Sarah shook her head. 'Nicole was sick and I didn't put in an appearance at all that week.'

'Yes, I remember. That explains it. Anyway, to get back to Rosa, we had a long chat over a cup of tea and a toasted bun and she suggested I should go and see her office which was only two streets away. I did so and she introduced me to her partner, Mr Snaith. It was while she was out of the room that he sang her praises to me and said how good she was. "As tip-top and fearless an advocate as you'll find in any magistrates court" were his words.' He beamed at Sarah as though she were a favourite niece, which was the way he had always regarded her. 'Would you like me to give Rosa a ring?'

'It's very kind of you, Jamie, but I think I ought to talk to Peter first.'

'Of course.' His expression became clouded. 'How's he taking things? He's scarcely said a word about what happened to anyone here.'

'He's desperately worried on my account. And when he gets worried he goes all silent.'

It was, indeed, true that he had said very little even to Sarah herself. He listened gravely to all her anguished outpourings and comforted her with hugs and caresses without showing any inclination to embark on a discussion of what the future might hold. She had accepted that this was a side of his nature; he had never found it easy to communicate, not even with a wife whom he obviously loved. Sarah had discovered early on in their marriage that he was an intensely private person and that certain subjects of a personal nature were taboo.

'He's a good chap, your husband,' Mr Jameson observed after a thoughtful pause. 'As long as you're satisfied he's all right, there's no need to worry.'

Something in his tone puzzled her. 'What exactly are you getting at?' she asked.

'Getting at? Nothing, my dear.'

'Has Peter said something to you?' she said suspiciously.

'Not a thing.'

28

'Done something then?'

Mr Jameson sucked in the end of his moustache, always an indication that something was bothering him, and frowned furiously at his desk. Then glancing up he said uncomfortably, 'If I'm merely being nosey forget I spoke, but what was Peter up to yesterday afternoon?'

It was Sarah's turn to put on a worried expression.

'I assume he was here correcting papers. Why?'

'Cecily Young saw him on Worthing station. She was going over to Brighton to shop and happened to spot him on the platform while she was waiting for her train. Nothing very remarkable about that except that he took great pains to avoid her and obviously hoped she hadn't seen him.'

'Did she speak to him?' she asked in a brittle tone.

'No. She decided to pretend she hadn't seen him. She thought it the most tactful thing to do in the circumstances.'

'But she told you?'

Mr Jameson nodded.

Cecily Young was an inveterate purveyor of news. Sarah quite liked her, but was careful never to tell her anything she didn't want broadcast around.

Mr Jameson let out a heavy sigh. 'I'm sorry now that I mentioned it,' he said, 'but I was puzzled and hoped you might provide the quick answer.' He paused. 'I'm sorry, my dear, if all I've done is to upset you. I'm sure there's a simple explanation. Peter will probably tell you of his own accord.'

And if he doesn't, Sara thought worriedly, do I ask him or not?

That evening, when Peter was in the kitchen giving her a casual hand in the preparation of supper, Sarah said, 'Jamie thinks I ought to consult a solicitor straightaway. He wants me to see someone he knows in London. A woman, the daughter of an old friend of his.' She paused, waiting for his reaction.

'Is it necessary at this stage?' he said in a quiet unemphatic tone.

'You're against it then?'

'What did you tell Jamie?'

29

'That I'd talk to you and see what you thought.'

He gave her a small, almost wistful, smile. 'I'd like you to do whatever will bring you most peace of mind, my darling one.'

'But you think we should still wait and see what's going to happen?'

'I'll go along with whatever you decide.'

'But I want you to help me decide. I want it to be our decision.'

'Then I suggest we wait.'

Because she had been largely living on her nerves the past few days, Sarah felt suddenly exasperated by his attitude. It was all very well his saying that he would go along with her decision, but it wasn't what she wanted. Surely he must realise what her feelings were in the matter and yet, when pressed, he gave an opposing view.

'Well I think I ought to see one,' she said defiantly. 'I'm certain to be charged with some offence and the sooner I take legal advice the better.'

He nodded slowly. 'O.K., we'll go and see Jamie's girlfriend.'

Sarah let out a sudden laugh. 'I don't think she's exactly that.'

He came across to where she was standing and put an arm round her shoulder, pulling her into his side.

'Make an appointment and we'll go and see the lady. If Jamie recommends her, she must be all right.'

For a while Sarah nestled against him. He was squarely built and strong so that she believed she could feel some of his strength flowing into her like an electric charge.

Without moving her head from against his shoulder she said in a tone of studied casualness, 'Somebody saw you at the station yesterday afternoon, Peter. What were you doing there?'

It seemed an age before he spoke, then all he said was, 'Cecily Young, I suppose.'

'Yes. She mentioned to Jamie she'd seen you on the platform.'

It seemed to Sarah that another interminable silence followed, though he continued to hold her closely to him. Finally she could bear it no longer and said in a whisper, 'Aren't you going to tell me what you were doing there?'

'I felt I had to get away on my own for an hour or two. Right away. I wanted to be in the open air and walk. Can you understand that, my darling Sarah?'

Relieved beyond measure to have his explanation, she nodded vigorously. 'Of course I understand, but why couldn't you have told me?'

'It seemed so selfish of me,' he said, obviously embarrassed.

'It wasn't selfish at all. It was perfectly normal. We've both been under an intolerable strain and it's all my fault.'

'You're not to say that. It's the fault of the young man who lost his life. I know he's dead, but it's still his fault.'

Sarah shivered, then said with a nervous little laugh, 'Where were you going to for your walk in the open air?'

'Arundel. The park there is so beautiful and peaceful – and has so many memories for me,'

'For me, too!'

It had been in Arundel Park on a perfect afternoon that he had proposed to her. It had been their favourite haunt for walks and picnics before Nicole was born.

It was not until she was getting undressed for bed that night that Sarah felt a sudden excruciating stab of doubt. The effect was so powerful that she had to sit down or she was sure she would have fallen. Fortunately Peter was in the bathroom at the time.

If Cecily Young had been waiting for a train to Brighton and Peter was bound for Arundel, they would never have been on the same platform as their destinations lay in opposite directions.

So what had he been doing at the station the previous afternoon?

Chapter 4

Rosa Epton thrived on hard work, without becoming anything as tiresome as a workaholic. She enjoyed criminal practice with its opportunity of advocacy and dealing with people under stress. Fortunately, her partner, Robin Snaith, didn't share her abhorrence of civil litigation and was prepared to handle such work of this nature as came the firm's way – mostly marital disputes and quarrels between landlords and tenants.

Rosa was now approaching thirty and had been with Robin, first as a clerk, then as a salaried solicitor and finally as a profit-sharing partner, for seven years. During that time she had firmly established herself in the profession and her reputation constantly brought her work from well outside the area in which the practice was rooted.

Recently, however, she had been bored. There had been no shortage of work, but none of her cases had really engaged her interest and to her this was vital. She needed to feel personally involved if she was to give of her best. She knew that lawyers were not meant to identify with their clients' causes – Robin had rubbed this in often enough when she was embarking on her career. They should, he told her, remain emotionally and intellectually detached, especially emotionally. But the fact was that her adrenalin flowed the better for a bit of personal feeling for a client or his cause.

When Mr Jameson telephoned and asked if one Sarah Atkins might come and seek her advice, she readily agreed, though without any noticeable quickening of her pulse. He told her no more than the barest details of what the matter was about and the appointment was duly made.

Rosa had no special liking for motoring cases which, in her view, abounded in technical evidence and generally lacked any human drama. However, the identity of the victim in this instance certainly promised to lift it out of the normal run.

Thus, a week to the day after Mr Jameson had discussed the matter with Sarah, she and Peter visited the office of Snaith and Epton in West London. For Sarah it had been an increasingly nerve-stretching week as she had continued to brood over Peter's explanation of what he had been doing at the railway station that afternoon. Neither of them had referred to it again, and as often as Sarah tried to put it out of her mind she failed.

On the other hand, Peter had been as solicitous and attentive as she could have wished and did everything possible to support his wife through a critical period. Sometimes Sarah was able to persuade herself that she had everything out of perspective and that he had not done anything which ought to disturb her peace of mind. At other times, however, it was as if she had a nagging toothache.

Their appointment with Rosa was for four o'clock. They arrived five minutes early and were shown immediately into her office. One look was sufficient to tell Rosa of the grim strain Sarah was undergoing. Her husband's concern for his wife was equally obvious, evidenced by the frequent anxious glances he cast in her direction.

'Jamie, Mr Jameson that is, spoke so highly of you,' Sarah said with a brave smile after the introductions had been made, 'so we decided to come and seek your advice straightaway. I don't imagine there's any need to ask if you've read about the case?'

Rosa gave a sympathetic nod. 'It would have been difficult not to read about it.'

'He's been made to sound such a perfect young man that a court's bound to be prejudiced against me from the outset,' Sarah observed bitterly. 'I'm sure his fans would be happy to lynch me here and now.'

'I'm sure a court won't let itself be prejudiced in that sort of way. Incidentally, have you heard anything further from the police?'

Sarah bit her lip. 'Yes, this morning. The analyst's report shows that I had an alcohol content in my blood of eighty-seven milligrammes per hundred millilitres of blood.' She spoke the words as if they were some dreaded formula she had been forced to learn by heart.

'That's only seven over the statutory limit,' Rosa remarked.

'But they'll still prosecute me, won't they?'

'Probably.'

'And I'll lose my licence?'

'Don't let's worry about that end of the case yet! Have you had any indication whether they intend prosecuting you for any other offence? For causing death by reckless driving, for example?'

'No. Sergeant Hibbert said the case might go to the Public Prosecutor for decision.'

Rosa looked thoughtful. 'I suppose it might in the circumstances. Anyway, tell me exactly what happened that evening!' She gave her visitors a smile of encouragement and pushed back her hair, which had fallen forward on either side of her face. 'I'd better get Stephanie to bring us in three cups of tea. She's our office Girl Friday and the only indispensable member of the staff. Then we'll begin.'

It took Sarah half an hour to tell her story while Rosa made quick, unobtrusive notes on a foolscap pad. When she reached the end Sarah turned to her husband and said, 'Have I left anything out, Peter?'

He shook his head gravely. 'Nothing.'

Turning to him Rosa remarked, 'And I take it, Mr Atkins, that you support everything your wife has said in so far as it falls within your own knowledge?'

'Yes.'

'In particular that Jonathan Cool's car was not showing any lights until after the accident had occurred?'

'I'm quite certain about that,' he said. 'We're both quite certain.'

'You'll have realised that it's a vital point,' Rosa observed. She stared thoughtfully at her notes for a few moments. 'If they were switched on afterwards, the presumption must be that it was done by Cheryl Peterson, which means she made a deliberate attempt to mislead the police. It further means that she must be ready to commit perjury, if necessary.' She paused. 'All in all, she doesn't sound a very nice girl. And from what you've told me, her father is as unscrupulous as his daughter.'

'He's doing all he can to stir things up against me,' Sarah remarked bitterly, 'and I've never even set eyes on him.'

'He obviously sees you as the person who's snatched a highly desirable son-in-law from under his nose.'

'They probably wouldn't have got married anyway!'

'Quite likely not. Jonathan can't have been exactly short of marriage options.' She shuffled her pages of notes. 'Do we accept that he really got out of the car in order to urinate?'

'That's what the girl has said.'

'I know. I suppose it's reasonable that somebody in his position wouldn't wish to be seen doing so in public and that's why he chose to stop in a particularly dark patch of mist and why he turned off the car lights. Presumably he was about to get back into his car when you collided with him. That fits in with the damage to your nearside wing and bumper.'

'The girl must have switched on the lights as soon as she realised what had happened.'

Rosa nodded. 'It shows considerable presence of mind.'

'It was a monstrous thing to do.'

Rosa gave a further nod. It occurred to her that if Cheryl Peterson was capable of conduct as heinous as that, she wasn't the sort of person who would be likely to crack in the witness box.

'At least it'll be two against one,' Sarah said with a note of defiance. 'I mean, Peter's and my word against hers.'

'I'm afraid evidence isn't generally weighed by numbers,' Rosa said. 'It's quality rather than quantity that counts.' She felt it would be heartless to add that a husband's evidence was scarcely regarded as independent in such a case.

There seemed nothing further to do until the police notified Sarah what they were proposing to do. In essence, this meant waiting to hear whether she was to be prosecuted for the offence of causing death by reckless driving.

'If they do proceed against you,' Rosa said as she steered the meeting to a close, 'it'll almost certainly be by way of summons. But even if you are arrested on warrant, you'll be immediately bailed, so don't let that add to your anxieties.' Observing Sarah's look of dismay she added in a sympathetic voice, 'Don't let the word arrest upset you.' She got up and came round her desk. 'We'll keep in touch, Mrs Atkins, and meanwhile I'll write to the police and inform them that you're my client. I'll also ask them to send me a copy of the statement you made. They're not likely to try and get a further one from you, but should they do so you can tell them that I've advised you not to say anything more without first speaking to me.'

After seeing her visitors out, Rosa returned to her room to sit down and think. She always liked to do this after interviewing a client. It was rather like retracing one's steps along a path in search of a mislaid object, though without necessarily knowing what one was looking for. She felt a particular need to think back over the interview that had just taken place.

One thing stood out a mile, there wasn't any room for honest mistake about the lights on Jonathan Cool's car. Somebody had to be lying. Either her client or Cool's girlfriend. Rosa never automatically accepted everything her clients told her for all too often they had a reason to lie. If not one hundred per cent falsehoods, certainly half-truths.

Sarah Atkins, however, hadn't given the impression of being a liar and there had been nothing in her story that had struck a false note. Morever, Rosa liked to think that Mr Jameson would not have taken the initiative in recommending her as a client unless she enjoyed his trust. He had certainly spoken very warmly of her as a person.

So, Rosa reflected, if she did accept everything Sarah had told her, what overall impression was she left with?

At this point she picked up her pen and began doodling on the pad of paper in front of her. Her doodles always took the form of strange heraldic beasts with exceptionally baleful expressions. Somebody had told her that they reflected her general suspicion of the world about her. It was certainly true that a criminal practice taught you to be sceptical of most things, in particular of people and their motives.

As she gazed at the creature she had drawn, she realised she had endowed it with the rather square features of Peter Atkins. It had not been a conscious act, even though he had been in her mind.

There was something about him that had puzzled her. He hadn't given the impression of being hen-pecked or downtrodden and yet he had been almost totally silent throughout the interview. He had sat with an intent expression, but left his wife to do all the talking. Admittedly, it was her story, but Rosa could think of few husbands who would not have intervened (even taken over) in such circumstances. When Rosa had invited his comment, he had readily agreed with his wife's account, in particular about the lights, or, rather, the absence of them, on Cool's car. He had shown no hesitation at all and had, indeed, spoken firmly and confidently.

'I'm quite certain about that,' he had said, adding for good measure, 'We're both quite certain.'

Rosa cast her mind back to what Mr Jameson had said about him over the phone. First-class chap, a thoroughly reliable member of my staff. One of the strong, silent types, but certainly nobody's fool. Sarah adores him and he's devoted to her and to little Nicole. Their engagement and marriage after such a short time took all our breaths away, but there's never been any sign of repenting at leisure. Of course, each of them was of an age to know what they wanted from life.

He had mentioned that Sarah was thirty-two and her husband twelve years older. Above all he had wanted Rosa to be satisfied that they carried his personal stamp of approval.

Well, if the police proceeded only on the breathalyser charge, it looked as though Sarah would have to plead guilty and the matter could be quickly disposed of in the magistrates' court. A fine and an inevitable suspension of her licence would be the outcome. Though there would still be a full-scale coroner's inquest to face.

If, on the other hand, she was charged with causing Cool's

death by reckless driving, the case would have to be tried by a jury at the crown court, and no way would there be a plea of guilty. Her ordeal would, moreover, be made worse by a blizzard of publicity, but that was something she would have to face when the time came.

Rosa shuffled her notes together and placed them in a folder on the outside of which she had written with a black, felt-tipped pen, 'ATKINS, Sarah'.

She felt she had just about reached the end of her brisk walk along memory lane when she recalled something further Mr Jameson had said on the phone. It had been when he was speaking of Peter Atkins.

'Take it from me, my dear, he's a sterling fellow. Don't be put off by his manner! He can sometimes appear a bit brusque.'

Rosa's impression had not been one of brusqueness so much as of still waters running deep.

Chapter 5

Stan Peterson would only reluctantly, even grudgingly, concede that he was not a fully qualified lawyer. He belonged to a breed of solicitor's clerk who liked to pose as all things to all people and give the impression that there were no strings he couldn't pull and no influence he couldn't exert. He had been with Henner & Co. for nearly thirty years and for most of that time had regarded himself as indispensable to the firm and God's special bonus to the clients with whom he dealt.

Like most solicitor's clerks who dealt with clients and the outside world, his effectiveness did very much depend on various ties, in particular with the police, in connection with the firm's criminal work.

He never lost any time in giving clients the impression that he was a confidant of all the important officers, who were flattered to respond to his beck and call. It need hardly be said that this view of the relationship was not generally reciprocated, though there were several who played along with him when it suited their own purpose.

It was to one of these that he addressed himself on the telephone the day after the Atkinses had been to see Rosa.

'That you, George? Stan here,' he said on being put through to P.C. George Whiting, a middle-aged, overweight officer who wore an indolent air but had the reputation of keeping both his ears to the ground at the same time. 'Anything you can tell me on the side about what's likely to happen?'

'Nothing,' P.C. Whiting replied with a sort of grunt.

'It's high time a decision was reached. I can't see what the

39

difficulty is. It's a clear enough case on Cheryl's evidence and all this delay isn't doing your image any good.'

'What do you mean, my image?' P.C. Whiting enquired raspingly.

'Not your personal image, George; the image of the decision-makers. If it had rested with you or me, we wouldn't have hesitated to slap on a charge of causing death by reckless driving. There's a plain case and it'll take a perverse jury to acquit.'

P.C. Whiting grunted again. 'These things always take time. It's not like it was some poor unknown sod who was killed. It was Jonathan Cool who copped it.'

'I don't get the logic of that, George.'

'Then forget it! Anyway, what's the rush where you're concerned?'

'All this delay is affecting Cheryl's health. She's not got over Jonathan's death and now she's waiting to know whether she'll have to face the ordeal of reliving it all over again when she gives evidence at the crown court. It's a terrible strain for the girl.'

'If she doesn't have to go to the crown court, she'll be required to give evidence at the inquest, so she'd better get used to the idea,' P.C. Whiting observed matter-of-factly.

'What's the general view among the police, George? In confidence, of course,' Stan Peterson said after a pause.

'Don't know that there is a general view.'

'What does Sergeant Hibbert think?'

'Haven't discussed the case with him,' P.C. Whiting remarked in a tone as unforthcoming as an empty jam jar.

The fact was that though he was often prepared to pass on items of inside information to Stan Peterson in exchange for all the double whiskies he drank at Henner & Co.'s expense, a toughly worded edict had come down from headquarters to the effect that officers were not to discuss the case with any of those (mostly press) seeking hot news and that any breach of this order would be regarded as a serious disciplinary offence. P.C. Whiting's immediate superior had gone further and said that his own officers should tie knots in their tongues rather than talk to

Stan Peterson.

'He's a pest at the best of times,' said the inspector in question austerely. 'Now he's a pest with a particularly large axe to grind.'

Realising that for some reason or another George Whiting was not in one of his more talkative moods at that moment, Stan changed his tactics.

'What about a drink at lunchtime, George?' he enquired affably.

'Could be,' Whiting said laconically.

'Usual place then?'

'No.'

'Somewhere different, you mean?'

'Yes.'

'O.K., I get you. What about the Passingham Arms?'

'That'll do.'

'See you there at half-past twelve.'

The firm for which Stan Peterson worked had two partners, Mr Douglas Henner and his son, Peter, who was still under thirty and who had not long joined. Stan had begun by treating the younger Henner with extreme condescension, but when 'Master Peter' (as he referred to him behind his back) made it clear which of them was the boss, Stan had beat a tactical retreat and now, so far as was possible, ignored the junior partner.

Following his conversation with P.C. Whiting, Stan went along to Mr Douglas Henner's room and, after a cursory knock on the door, entered without waiting for a reply. It was the nicest room in the building, situated on the first floor and overlooking some gardens. Palatine Crescent was a prime location for professional offices and Henner & Co. had been there since Mr Douglas Henner's father had founded the firm just after World War I.

Mr Henner looked up from his desk and sighed. Though used to his senior clerk's interruptions, he did secretly agree with his son that Stan Peterson was perhaps allowed a bit too much licence.

'Just been talking to the police about that case,' Stan announced. There was no need for Mr Henner to enquire which case as Stan had scarcely spoken of anything else since the fateful evening. 'I told them I thought it disgraceful that it was taking so long to reach a decision and that their procrastination was undermining my daughter's health.'

Mr Henner squirmed slightly. 'I hope you made it clear, Stan, that you were speaking in a personal capacity. After all, we have no status in the matter as a firm.'

'Not yet. It's very likely, however, that I shall have to brief counsel to look after Cheryl's interests.'

Mr Henner gave a further uneasy squirm. 'Isn't that a bit premature?'

'Provided that woman is charged with causing death by reckless driving, it won't be necessary,' Stan said in his most portentous voice. 'But if the D.P.P. or the police shirk their responsibility, then there'll be a full-scale inquest and Cheryl will have to be represented.'

'I'd be glad, Stan, if you'd have a word with me before you take any action in the firm's name.'

Stan nodded as if acknowledging a formality. 'It may be,' he went on, 'that if the authorities don't prefer a charge, I shall start a private prosecution.'

Mr Henner jumped. 'That would call for the most careful consideration,' he said anxiously.

'Oh, I'd not take any action without consulting counsel,' Stan assured him airily.

'Even so. . .'

'Anyway, I hope it won't get to that stage.'

'I hope not either,' Mr Henner said in a fervent tone.

Stan glanced at his watch.

'I'd better be off. Want to call in at the court and collect a witness summons in the Birtley case. I'll be back in the office this afternoon.'

Mr Henner observed his clerk's departure with a sigh. Whatever his son, Peter, might say, the firm would be lost should Stan Peterson be suddenly removed by a thunderbolt – or even by a passing car. He was a thoroughly efficient and reliable outdoor

42

clerk, even if he was the possessor of an outsize ego.

Mr Henner decided it would be best not to tell Peter what had just transpired in his room. His reaction would be predictable. He would expostulate and say that there were better clerks to be found at the end of the pier on a rainy afternoon and that it was high time they brought one in out of the wet and trained him.

The incompatibility of junior partner and senior clerk was something Mr Henner felt he could do without in his remaining years. He was a peaceable man who detested friction around him. A good court battle, on the other hand, was always to be relished.

With a further and yet deeper sigh he turned his attention back to the will he had been drafting when Stan had breezed in and interrupted him.

P.C. Whiting took a swig of his second large scotch, leaned more heavily against the bar and said, 'I overheard Sergeant Hibbert talking to headquarters as I was leaving.'

'About the case?' Stan asked eagerly.

'Sounded like it,' P.C. Whiting said as he took a further swig and gazed moodily around the bar. 'I'll be damned if it isn't Sid the stoat over there,' he suddenly exclaimed, focusing his gaze on a small rodent-faced man sitting by himself in a corner. 'He can't have been out long. Got a couple of years last time. Indecent assault on schoolgirls. Not a client of yours, is he?'

Stan shook his head. 'No, but he looks like a member of the mackintosh brigade.'

'A member for life at that! He'll be inside again before long. Can't keep his hands to himself. Mind you, all he ever wants is a quick feel and a pat and the girls were the sort to do anything for a bit of pocket money. Fourteen-year-olds with minds like open sewers.'

'What was Sergeant Hibbert saying?' Stan asked a trifle impatiently.

'Not a bad drop of scotch this,' P.C. Whiting remarked, draining his glass and pushing it along the counter in Stan's direction.

'You were about to tell me what Hibbert was saying,' Stan

reminded him after the glass had been replenished.

'He was asking when a decision was likely to be reached in the Cool case. Whoever he was talking to apparently told him there were wheels within wheels.'

'What's that supposed to mean?' Stan asked sharply.

'Search me! But you know how it is in these cases that are all publicity. Different considerations come into play.'

'I don't mind telling you, George, that if proceedings aren't taken against that woman for causing Jonathan's death, I'm prepared to launch a private prosecution. It's a citizen's right and I'd owe it to Cheryl.'

P.C. Whiting blinked in surprise. 'I've always thought that folk who instituted private prosecutions must have more money than sense,' he said with a slight belch.

'Money would be of secondary importance,' Stan retorted in a lofty tone. 'Somebody's got to see that justice is done,' he went on determinedly. 'And in this instance. I'd regard it as my duty.'

P.C. Whiting's only comment was a further belch. 'I'd better have a sandwich,' he said.

Stan stood, glass in hand, frowning thoughtfully for a while. 'And I don't like the sound of wheels within wheels,' he said at length. 'If there's any funny business going on behind the scenes, I'll see it's brought out into the open.' He drained his glass and put it down. 'I'll keep in touch with you, George. Meanwhile, let me know if you hear anything of interest.'

'Don't try and drag me into anything, that's all!'

'You know you can trust me.'

P.C. Whiting nodded. 'One good turn deserves another,' he observed without particular relevance. Three double whiskies at lunchtime were liable to produce non sequiturs. He thought he had better go down to the shore and breathe in a few lungfuls of bracing sea air before returning to the station.

Stan, for his part, left the pub in a mood of incipient indignation, which was something near his norm. He found much in life about which to wax indignant and demand redress. In view of what George Whiting had said to him he decided he would get in touch with a local reporter of his acquaintance. It was time to start stirring the pot more vigorously.

Chapter 6

Sarah continued to live in a state of suspended animation. She spent more time than usual playing with Nicole and threw herself with feverish energy into a succession of domestic chores. Cupboards and drawers were turned out, carpets were vacuumed twice over and the kitchen stove was taken apart and cleaned as never before, all in an effort to forget the cloud that hung over her life. All her endeavour, however, was only intermittently successful.

Peter was exemplary in his caring way, though whenever she tried to talk to him about what might happen to her, he seemed singularly bereft of words.

'Don't let's meet trouble halfway,' he would say firmly and change the subject. Though he made love to her as passionately and imaginatively as before, Sarah sensed that something had happened to them. Most of the time she was able to persuade herself that it was her fault; that her perspective had become hopelessly distorted. This was particularly so when her mind dwelt on what he had been doing at Worthing station that afternoon. Several times she had come close to broaching the subject again, but had shied away at the last moment. She was sure there was an innocent explanation and yet. . .

It was at night as she lay beside his sleeping form in bed that her thoughts really went on the rampage. She would feel guilt-ridden at having been the cause of the death of a talented and seemingly likeable young man. Her feeling of guilt had nothing to do with what the law might or might not say on the subject, but was a piece of morbid self-indulgence. On these occasions she almost hoped she *would* be prosecuted, if only to purge her of her masochistic feelings.

It was towards the end of the week after she and Peter had visited Rosa Epton that they went to the theatre in Brighton. Mr Jameson had bought the tickets without telling them.

'It'll do you both good to have an evening out,' he had said heartily. 'I'm told it's a hilarious play so go and enjoy yourselves.'

Sarah had been reluctant to go, but Peter, who didn't normally care for the theatre, said Jamie would be hurt if they didn't go.

In the event the evening was anything but a success. The theatre was half-empty and the 'riot of laughter' promised by the billboards outside was no more than a self-conscious trickle of titters. Peter sat glumly at her side and made an unceremonious dash for the bar as soon as the curtain fell on the first act. Sarah followed him, wishing to goodness they had stayed at home. When they emerged from the theatre at the end it was pouring with rain and she went ankle-deep in muddy water in one of the car park's artfully sited potholes.

They arrived back home around eleven-thirty to be told by Rosemary, the baby-sitter, that a Miss Epton had phoned and would Mrs Atkins please call her as soon as she came in.

'You speak to her, Peter,' Sarah said, giving her husband an anxious glance.

'I'll drive Rosemary home first,' he replied. 'I'll be back in ten minutes and it can wait until then. Now, don't worry, my darling,' he said in a quick aside as he followed the girl out of the room.

It seemed to Sarah that he was scarcely out of the door before the phone began to ring. Only fear that it might awaken Nicole forced her to answer it.

'Mrs Atkins? It's Rosa Epton. Did you get my message?'

'Yes, but we've only just got back and I was about to phone you. As a matter of fact my husband's taking our baby-sitter home and I thought I'd wait till he returned before speaking to you.' Her words came in a nervous gush. Anything to forestall the moment of finding out the reason for Rosa's call. It couldn't possibly be anything reassuring at that hour of the night.

'Have the police been in touch with you, Mrs Atkins?' Rosa

asked.

'The police? No. No, I've not heard a thing from them,' Sarah said breathlessly.

'I asked Sergeant Hibbert to let me speak to you first, but I thought he might jump the gun. I'm afraid you're going to be prosecuted for the offence of causing death by reckless driving. I don't expect it'll come as that much of a surprise to you. You may even feel relieved that the waiting for a decision is over.'

'But I wasn't driving recklessly,' Sarah said with sudden indignation.

'I know, but the case against you is obviously based on what the girl has said. Now that proceedings have been launched we shall get a copy of her statement and see exactly what she *has* said. Anyway, I've asked Sergeant Hibbert if I can bring you along to the police station tomorrow morning when you will be charged, and he's agreed to that course. It's the most civilised way of dealing with the situation, seeing that they didn't want to proceed by way of summons, and will, I hope, save greater embarrassment. I was particularly anxious that the police shouldn't come driving up to your door in full view of the neighbours.'

'Did Sergeant Hibbert phone *you?*' Sarah asked in an effort to sound intelligent.

'No, I happened to ring him just before I left my office this evening and he'd just had a message from headquarters. I tried to call you immediately, but was told you'd gone to the theatre, so I called him back and got him to agree to my proposal.' Rosa paused before adding wryly, 'From what you'd told me he sounded a reasonable officer and so it was one of those occasions for soft soap rather than boxing gloves. I'll drive down early tomorrow and we'll go along to the station together.'

'Will it be all right for my husband to come too?'

'Of course. I'll be with you soon after nine, Mrs Atkins.'

As soon as she heard Peter open the front door, Sarah dashed out into the hall and threw herself at him. He listened to what she told him and hugged her tightly in silence for a while. 'I wonder when the case is likely to be heard,' he said at length.

Always one for the practical comment, Sarah reflected ruefully as she clung to him.

'I don't expect the actual trial at the crown court will be for months,' she said. 'But I imagine I'll appear before the magistrates immediately and be let out on bail.' She gave a small shiver. 'I'm dreading all the publicity, Peter. There are sure to be photographers around.'

'Don't fret about it, my darling,' he murmured in a soothing voice.

'You'll have to phone Jamie first thing in the morning and tell him you won't be in till later in the day. He'll understand.'

When he spoke next it seemed to Sarah that his voice came from a hundred miles away. 'It's not easy for me to take time off tomorrow,' he said quietly.

'But Peter. . .' she exclaimed in dismay.

'Ssh! Just listen to me, my darling,' he said, placing a finger over her lips to quell her words. 'I've promised to give extra tuition to Antonio tomorrow. He has his exam at the Institute in London the next day and I gave him my promise weeks ago.'

'Surely he'd understand?'

'It wouldn't be fair on him.'

'So it's more important to give him tuition than go with me to the police station, is that it?' Sarah observed bitterly.

'It's just that I think you can manage better without me tomorrow than he can. After all, Miss Epton will be with you and there's nothing I could do.'

'You could give me much needed moral support.' She paused. 'Let me speak to Jamie in the morning! I know he'll understand and be able to get someone else to help Antonio.'

He shook his head. 'No,' he said firmly.

'You're deserting me in my hour of need,' Sarah said, at the same time despising herself for resorting to emotional blackmail.

'You're overwrought, my darling,' he said, kissing her tenderly on the forehead. 'It's natural, but everything's going to be all right. I shall be thinking of you so hard tomorrow that you'll feel my presence beside you even though I'm not there but with the hairy Antonio.'

49

It seemed to Sarah that the night had almost passed before she fell asleep. Her mind was in turmoil as she sought to rationalise Peter's attitude. But however hard she tried she always came back to the cruel fact that he was deserting her. Could he not realise how much she wanted him at her side, even if there was nothing practical he could do?

She was now sure that something had happened to him. But what? Outwardly he was the same person he had always been, but it was as if a soundproof glass panel had been lowered between them, cutting off vital communication.

When sleep did eventually come to her, she had a confused dream in which Peter and Cecily Young were playing hide and seek on Worthing station.

'My husband won't be coming with us,' Sarah said as she and Rosa sat with cups of coffee in the living-room. Rosa had just arrived and Peter was upstairs getting ready to go to Mr Jameson's. Nicole, for once in a grizzling mood as though she sensed something was wrong, had already been parked with a neighbour. 'He's got an important session with one of his students and can't get away.'

Sarah's tone told Rosa that something had happened between husband and wife, but she was left to speculate what.

'There's nothing he could do, anyway,' she remarked with a small smile.

'I'd been hoping for his moral support.'

'Perhaps I'll be able to supply that instead. I'm afraid you must be prepared to run the gauntlet with the photographers. I've asked Sergeant Hibbert to try and get us in and out of court without any additional aggravation, but how much he can, or will, do remains to be seen. The press shouldn't, of course, know anything until you've appeared in court and been remanded, but they always find these things out in advance. It's their job and they have their spies everywhere.'

Peter came into the room and greeted Rosa. 'Look after my wife for me, Miss Epton,' he said as they shook hands. 'She's probably told you that I can't accompany you this morning.'

'So I understand. As soon as the prosecution has served the statements on us – that is, the statements of all the witnesses on whom they are going to rely – we must have a further meeting and discuss the next step.'

'Of course,' he said gravely, 'I can make myself available almost any time.'

'My guess is that the vital issue is going to be whether or not there were any lights showing on Cool's car and your evidence will be most important in backing up your wife's.'

'I realise that. Well, if you'll excuse me, I'd better go.' He walked across to his wife and bent over to kiss her. 'Remember, I'll be with you in spirit, my darling. Phone as soon as you get home. I'll be worrying until I hear that everything's all right.'

'What is all right?' Sarah said with a small bleak smile. 'That I've not been locked up in a cell?'

Rosa felt that her intervention was required to disperse the sudden air of tension.

'The court will probably release you on bail on your own recognisance,' she said quickly, 'but if they do require a surety, do you have anyone in mind?'

'I'm sure Mr Jameson would stand,' Peter said.

'He's already offered to,' Sarah remarked. 'I thought I'd told you.'

Peter turned and walked slowly towards the door. He hovered there a moment as if to see whether his wife would follow him out of the room for a private word of farewell. But she made no effort to get up and he blew her a shy kiss and disappeared.

Sarah had been inside the local magistrates' court on two previous occasions, the first when one of the school's students, a Moroccan, was charged with shop-lifting and the second when a Finnish student was up for being drunk and disorderly and pitting his strength against that of a traffic light. The traffic light had come off second best.

On each occasion she had gone along to speak on behalf of the defendant to save him from something worse than might be expected. On each she was successful and had left the court with

51

a feeling of smug satisfaction.

How different it was on this, her third, appearance! As she stood in the dock and stared fixedly ahead, she was scarcely aware of her surroundings. The court had assumed an atmosphere of total unreality. The three magistrates facing her might have come from a different planet. There were two men in dark suits and a woman in a simple navy blue dress. All three wore alert but grave expressions as though determined to do their duty whatever the consequences.

The young clerk of the court read out the charge in a faintly nonchalant tone as though bored by all the legal rigmarole. Sergeant Hibbert asked for a remand and said there was no objection to bail and Rosa asked that restrictions on reporting should remain in force for the time being. She also applied for legal aid on behalf of her client.

The magistrates bent their heads together in whispered consultation before the Chairman announced the court's agreement to all that had been asked of it.

The reporters, who had filled every space, now headed for the exit like exuberant fans at the end of a football match. Amongst them was Stan Peterson, eager to hold his own court outside.

'That was the worst part of all,' Sarah said vehemently after she and Rosa had run the gauntlet to Rosa's car which had been parked in a side road. 'They have no finer feelings at all.'

'I agree, though they wouldn't be much good at their job if they had. It's unfortunate that news-gathering invariably means trampling over people's susceptibilities. Anyway we're free of them for the time being,' she added as she accelerated away. 'The trouble with so many of these new courts is that they're sited like block-houses – often look like them too – so that you can't get near without being observed.'

The building they had just left was a corner site and as familiar in appearance to Rosa as one shoe box is to another. It was compact and functional where the older court houses squandered space and made a speciality of discomfort.

'Which way do I go?' Rosa enquired as they came up to a crossroads.

'Depends where you're heading for,' Sarah remarked with a wan smile. 'If you turn left you get into Swift Road where Mr Jameson's is.'

'Why don't we call there then?' Rosa said.

'If you can spare the time. I'd like to tell Peter what's happened.'

'Of course. And I can pay my respects to Mr Jameson and thank him for sending me a client.'

'It's that large house on the right,' Sarah said a moment later after they had made the turn.

'And miracle upon miracle I can actually park. There's not even a single yellow line to ignore.'

She got out, locked the car and followed Sarah up the drive to the house. There was a solid wooden porch door which was open and beyond it the front door itself that had a large upper panel made up of diamond-shaped pieces of coloured glass. This door was also unlocked and Sarah led the way in. As they entered, Mr Jameson emerged from a room on their right.

'Sarah, my dear!' he exclaimed. 'And Miss Epton, too! Or may I now call you Rosa? Come into my study and tell me how things went this morning. I thought it must be you when I heard the car pull up outside and somebody came in without ringing the bell.' He fussed about them until they were seated and then departed in search of coffee.

'He's treating me as if I'd just come out of hospital,' Sarah remarked. 'It's a wonder he didn't put a rug over my knees. I wonder where Peter is? I suppose I'd better not go looking for him. He'd be put out if I suddenly barged in on him without warning.'

'I expect Mr Jameson will tell him you're here.'

Rosa glanced about her. The room lacked only an aspidistra to complete its Victorian appearance. There was bric-a-brac everywhere and embroidered anti-macassars on all the chairs. Mr Jameson's desk in the bay window was piled haphazardly high with paper so that looking for anything would be a daunting task.

Observing Rosa's glance, Sarah said, 'I'm the only person who could keep his desk tidy. Just look at it now!'

'He's probably one of those people who finds things more easily when they're in a mess.'

'That's what he always says.'

The door opened and he re-appeared bearing a tray with three cups of coffee on it.

'Does Peter know I'm here, Jamie?' Sarah asked as she took the tray from him.

'No, but he'll be back at any minute.'

'Back! I thought he was supposed to be giving Antonio some extra coaching.'

'He is,' said Mr Jameson. 'But as it was such a nice day he thought it would be a good idea to go down to the sea front. He felt it would relax Antonio more than sitting in a classroom.'

'Is that what Peter said?' Sarah asked with a note of incredulity.

'Yes. I expect they've had a brisk walk and then sat in one of the shelters out of the wind.' He turned to Rosa. 'Even with the sun shining it can be quite bracing on the promenade at this time of year.'

It was apparent to Rosa that Sarah was disconcerted by what she had just heard and was uncertain how to react. The undercurrent in the relationship between husband and wife was manifesting itself again.

Mr Jameson glanced toward the grandfather clock that stood in one corner of the room. 'I'm sure they'll be back very soon,' he repeated.

In a slightly ominous tone Sarah said, 'Tell me, Jamie, would it have upset things very much if Peter had taken the morning off?'

Mr Jameson frowned and gave his moustache a nervous tug. 'He's very keen that Antonio should pass tomorrow. He's our first student to take this particular exam and he's also one of Peter's star pupils.'

'I daresay, but if Peter had told you he wanted to go with me to court, couldn't you have made some other arrangement for Antonio?'

'You sound resentful, my dear, it's not like you. Peter can't have realised how much it meant to you. He probably just felt he could be more use here. Don't be cross with him!'

Sarah said nothing further and Rosa sipped her coffee in the uncomfortable silence that ensued. After a few moments, Mr Jameson got up from his desk chair and went to look out of the window.

'I think I recognise the top of Antonio's head over the hedge,' he said with forced cheerfulness. 'I knew they'd be back soon. I'll go and tell Peter you're here and then I'll take Rosa on a conducted tour of the school.'

He left the room and they could hear a murmur of voices in the hall. A moment later he returned.

'Peter will be here in a minute,' he said. 'Apparently he stopped to make a phone call on the way back.'

'A phone call!' Sarah exclaimed in a tone laden with suspicion. 'Why couldn't he have made it here when he returned?'

'You can ask him that yourself, my dear,' Mr Jameson observed in a matter-of-fact voice.

'Where's he making this phone call?' Sarah persisted.

'At the call-box outside the sub-post-office, I gather. He told Antonio to go on ahead. If he'd known you were here I'm sure he wouldn't have dallied.'

Sarah lapsed into a frowning silence. Rosa, meanwhile, found herself increasingly intrigued. From the outset Peter Atkins had struck her as a man of slight mystery. On the surface he was everything a good husband should be, but there was something odd about his manner. It seemed, moreover, that his wife was only finding this out for the first time. But what was there about a fatal road accident to cause him to act strangely? Admittedly his wife was the driver and the victim was a household name, but Rosa couldn't help feeling there must be some other factor hidden deep beneath the surface.

Rosa was aware that Mr Jameson's guided tour was no more than an excuse to leave Sarah and Peter on their own for fifteen minutes or so. In fact there was little to see as one classroom looked much like another and the students' reading-room resembled something between play-school and a dentist's waiting room.

Peter had returned about ten minutes after Antonio and Mr Jameson had hurried out into the hall to tell him of his wife's presence. He had entered the study wearing an expression of anxious solicitude and gone immediately over to where Sarah was sitting. She lifted a hand in a somewhat wan and rueful greeting.

'Am I happy to see you, my darling!' he had said. At which point Rosa and Mr Jameson removed themselves and began their tour of the school.

'I've now been running this place for over fifty years,' Mr Jameson said with a reminiscing sigh as he and Rosa stood aimlessly in a small empty classroom. 'I'm sorry your father never got down for a visit.'

'The ten-mile drive into Hereford was the limit of his travelling after my mother's death. And he'd always hated London.'

'I know how he must have felt.'

'But you told me when we met in town that you still went cycling in France every summer.'

'Yes, but I've gone soft. I now stop at inns, whereas I used to take a small tent and camp out.' He glanced furtively towards the door. 'I'm so distressed about Sarah. The accident obviously wasn't her fault and yet she now finds herself caught up in the machinations of the law. It's putting a great strain on both her and Peter.'

'Yes, I realise that. I'm afraid criminal cases are apt to have unwelcome effects on those involved.' Rosa paused and went on. 'I get the impression that her husband is finding it difficult to cope with the situation.'

A frown settled over Mr Jameson's face. 'And yet in the normal way he's such a staunch and unflappable sort of person. Quite frankly, Rosa, he has me puzzled. I don't know what to make of his recent behaviour.'

'What's his background?' Rosa asked curiously.

'He's never talked about his early life; at least, not to me. I know he was born in London and I recall his once giving me the impression that he was orphaned while still a baby and was brought up in an institution. But, as I say, it's not something he's given to talking about. I've always assumed that he'd had an unhappy childhood he'd sooner forget.'

'Does he have any family?'

'None that I'm aware of. I presume Sarah knows his family background.'

'How did he come to apply for a teaching post here?' Rosa said, her curiosity further aroused.

'I'd advertised in various trade papers and he was by far the best of the applicants. I took up his references, which were excellent, and that was that.'

'Had he been teaching before he joined you?'

'Yes. One of his referees was the retired headmistress of a school in North London and she gave him a glowing testimonial. As, indeed, I now would myself.' He paused and blew through his moustache. 'I've always believed that meeting Sarah was a turning point in his life. For the first time he felt happy and secure.' He gave Rosa a sudden smile. 'I suppose we all have friends who keep part of their lives to themselves. It's man's nature. Most of us were born with a sense of privacy and reserve. And a good thing too! I can't stand people who tell you everything about themselves almost before you've finished shaking hands.'

Rosa glanced at her watch. 'I ought to start making tracks for London. I wonder if Mrs Atkins wants a lift home or if she'll wait here until her husband's ready to leave.'

'Let's go and find out,' Mr Jameson said, as if welcoming an excuse to move out of the classroom in which they had been talking.

When they got back to the study, they found Peter and Sarah sitting on the sofa like a pair of shy, young lovers. They were holding hands and while he was talking earnestly to her in a low voice, she was gazing into the fireplace. Her expression was one of sad resignation, as though she had given up hoping for the best.

As soon as Rosa mentioned her wish to start back, Peter suggested that his wife should stay and have lunch at the school. She seemed to hesitate for a moment, but then nodded her

57

agreement.

'We'll have a meeting as soon as the statements have been served,' Rosa said as she shook hands with Sarah. 'Meanwhile don't hesitate to get in touch with me if you wish.'

Mr Jameson accompanied her out of the room.

'I take it there's no possibility of Sarah being sent to prison, is there?' he said as they reached the front door.

'I hope she won't even be convicted,' Rosa replied. 'But if she is, I would expect a fine at the most, also the loss of her licence which'll probably be the worst part.' She gave Mr Jameson a steady look. 'From what she and her husband have told me of the accident, she should be acquitted of the main charge. What we don't yet know, of course, is what Cheryl Peterson has told the police. The charge must be principally based on her evidence.'

Mr Jameson made a tut-tutting noise. 'I suppose it's inevitable you get divergent views in a motoring case,' he said.

'You get more perjury than in any other sort,' Rosa remarked.

Mr Jameson's expression turned to one of shock.

'Not deliberate perjury, surely you're not saying that?'

'Perjury comes in all shades from pale grey to deepest black in practically every motoring case,' Rosa replied.

Chapter 7

Rosa was agreeably surprised when a week later she received a file containing the statements of all the prosecution witnesses. Apart from Cheryl Peterson they comprised the evidence of police officers, doctors and other experts, such as plan-drawers and vehicle examiners. But Cheryl remained the only lay witness of any consequence.

Rosa had not expected to receive them so soon and hadn't even reached the point of raising hell, something she was used to having to do. They came from police headquarters in Worthing under cover of a compliments slip and Rosa assumed that Sergeant Hibbert had been behind their despatch, though obviously he would not have sent them without the approval of someone further up the hierarchical ladder. At all events their source of origin seemed to confirm that the D.P.P.'s department was no longer interested in the case, even though it might have advised on the question of proceedings.

It was therefore to her further surprise when she received a phone call the next day from one of the Assistant Directors in the department.

'Miss Epton? This is Philip Godwin of the D.P.P.'s department. I understand the police have sent you a bundle of statements in the case of Mrs Sarah Atkins. . . you know, the Jonathan Cool case. . . have you received them yet?'

'They came yesterday.'

'Ah! Well, I'm afraid they were sent in error, Miss Epton. The police shouldn't have served them on you. There's been a bit of a misunderstanding. In fact, we're assuming responsibility for the conduct of the case and we'll be serving a set of statements in due

59

course.'

'What's wrong with the set I've got?'

'Probably nothing, but it might be better if you sent them to us and then we can start afresh. I hope that's not putting you to too much bother.'

'I'll post them to you today,' Rosa said pleasantly, having already decided that she would first copy them.

'That's fine then. I'm afraid these things are apt to happen when there's more than one finger in the pie. Please don't think I'm criticising the police for having jumped the gun! As I said, there's been a simple misunderstanding.'

The file of statements had lain under Rosa's gaze as she spoke and for a while she continued to stare at its slender contents.

'Curiouser and curiouser,' she murmured to herself. Or was it all as innocent as the Assistant Director had been at pains to make out?

She pulled the file towards her and opened it at Cheryl Peterson's statement, which she had already read several times. It was the linchpin of the prosecution's case, as she had known it would be.

Her full name, the statement told Rosa, was Cheryl Sonia Peterson, she was eighteen years old and lived with her parents at 8 Melford Avenue, Worthing, and worked at a beauty salon in West Worthing. It continued:

'I had known Jonathan Cool for three months and we had become close friends. I used to visit him in London, but more often he used to drive down to Worthing and we would go out together. On Friday, 29th October 1982, he came down in the evening and picked me up in his car at my home. His car is a Lotus. We went to Fables at Goring-on-Sea. It's a club owned by an old friend of Jonathan's called Micky Spicer. He and Jonathan used to be members of the same pop group. We often went there. We had dinner and then sat talking till just after ten o'clock. Jonathan only had Coca-Cola to drink as he never touched alcohol. I had a small vodka and lime before dinner and a Pimms Number One with my meal. I didn't have anything else to drink that evening. When we left the club there were patches of mist about. Jonathan was going to drop me off at my home as he had to be up early the next morning for a rehearsal of a Christmas T.V. show in which he was making a guest appearance. On the way back he stopped the car where there were some bushes at the side of the road. He had forgotten to go to the toilet before we left Fables and he needed to answer a call of nature. That's why he stopped. It was a bit misty at that point so he switched on the yellow hazard lights before he got out. I couldn't say exactly how long he was away from the car, but it could have been about two minutes. I saw him come round the front of the car to get back in when I heard another car coming up behind very fast. I could tell it was fast by the noise the engine was making. The next thing was that this other car struck Jonathan just as he was about to open the driver's door. I would say this other car was going too fast for the weather conditions. I am quite sure that Jonathan's car was showing all the proper lights at the time; namely its red tail lights and the yellow hazard lights that blink on and off. I could see their reflection from my seat. I didn't actually see the red tail lights on at that stage but I know they were working when we left Fables and they were never switched off. As soon as the accident happened I got out and rushed to where Jonathan was lying in the road. I was hysterical and don't really remember much else. It was all a blur, a sort of nightmare. I know that the driver of the other car was a woman as I saw her face through the windscreen. I believe I shouted that she had killed Jonathan. Later I was taken into someone's house and my father came and fetched me home. He sent for the doctor who gave me a sedative. I hold a driving licence, and I have occasionally driven Jonathan's Lotus. I can't think why the woman driving the other car didn't see our car. I don't think there's anything further I can add. I am willing to attend court and give evidence any time I am required. Everything I have said in this statement is the truth.'

Rosa made a derisive sound as she read the final sentence. It wasn't even a case of half-truths and multiple self-deception.

She turned the pages until she reached Sergeant Hibbert's statement, the first part of which dealt with his attendance at the scene, followed by his interviewing Sarah at the police station and finally with her being charged with causing death by reckless driving and have alcohol in her blood over the legal limit.

It was, as Rosa had already noted, only seven milligrammes over, which was infinitesimal compared with some of the people she had represented in court on that particular charge. In her own record book was a client who had driven with two hundred and fifty milligrammes over the limit. It had followed his being jilted by the girl he loved, a mitigating factor which failed to save him from a heavy fine and the loss of driving licence for two years.

Sergeant Hibbert described the weather at the time as a damp mist which varied in density and which had started forming around eight o'clock in the evening. At the scene of the accident he had found a Lotus car, registration number CYR 82V, parked about a foot from the kerb at a point where shrubs and bushes separated the road from the footpath. The car had its red tail lights showing, its front sidelights and its yellow hazard warning lights fore and aft. It was visible, he said, from twenty yards away coming from the rear. The nearest street light was not working so that the immediate vicinity was a pool of darkness. He described the damage to Sarah's car as being to the nearside end of the front bumper and to the wing on that side. It was this part of her car which had struck Cool and thrown him forward on to the road. The impact appeared to have taken place when the two cars were virtually parallel with one another. He had been unable to find any independent witnesses to the accident.

The pathologist who had conducted the post-mortem examination on Cool stated that he had died from severe brain damage caused by his head coming into violent contact with the hard surface of the road. His other injuries consisted of a deep laceration to his left leg below the knee where the car had struck him and bruising in the region of his left thigh, probably caused by the wing of the car before he was thrown forward on to the ground.

It seemed clear enough that, in one sense, Cool's death was pure misfortune. If his head had not struck the road in the exact manner it did, he would probably have survived, for his other injuries in no way contributed to his death.

Rosa laid down her pencil and sat back. The battlelines were clearly drawn. It was going to be a straight contest between Sarah and Cheryl Peterson. It was one thing to be certain that Cheryl was a blatant and determined liar, another to prove it in court. Her effective cross-examination would be absolutely vital and would require finesse and skill. If conducted in a maladroit fashion, it could gain her sympathy and alienate the jury against Sarah.

The issue could hardly be more straightforward, yet Rosa felt a burden of responsibility as seldom before.

Her somewhat sombre thoughts were interrupted by the telephone.

'I have Mr Atkins on the line,' Stephanie announced when Rosa lifted the receiver. 'He's in a public call-box. Shall I put him through?'

'Yes.'

'Miss Epton? It's Peter Atkins. I wonder if I might come and see you sometime tomorrow?'

'Of course. I'll be free in the afternoon. I take it you mean you and your wife?'

'No. I'd like to come on my own. In fact, Sarah doesn't know I'm getting in touch with you. What time shall I come?'

'Three-thirty?'

'Thank you,' he said in his studiously polite way and immediately rang off.

Rosa had been so taken by surprise that it was only now she began to question whether she had been right to agree to a meeting. After all, it wasn't as if he were her client. She had been intending to telephone Sarah and tell her of the latest developments, namely her receipt of the statements and the D.P.P.'s assumption of responsibility for the prosecution. Now, however, she hesitated to do so.

She felt not only puzzled, but strangely apprehensive.

Chapter 8

The next morning Rosa drove to court to defend one of their firm's most loyal and regular clients, a young man named Terry who was seldom out of trouble but who retained a flattering faith in Rosa's ability to rescue him from the more dire consequences of his behaviour.

Though his conduct was unfailingly reprehensible, Rosa, for her part, had always had a soft spot for him, his rebellious streak seeming to strike a sympathetic chord in her own nature.

On this occasion he was up for assaulting a police officer, who had stopped him in the early hours of the morning on his way home from an all-night launderette and demanded to see the contents of the blue plastic bag he was carrying. Though it contained nothing more suspicious than an assortment of now clean garments, he had resented the officer's tone and manner and had given him a smart kick on the shin before legging it down the street. Misfortune, however, overtook him, as so often before, when he slipped on the pavement and went flying. The police were later piously to assert that his black eye and various other bruises were attributable to his fall, and certainly not as a result of any unofficial retribution at the police station, as he alleged.

It was a familiar story and counter story that Rosa had often heard before. In her experience courts displayed a public preference in not believing that the police would ever assault those in their custody.

As she weaved her way through the morning traffic, she turned her mind to Peter Atkins's coming visit later in the day. On the whole she felt slightly more optimistic about it than she had the previous evening. It could, she reasoned, only help to explain and

64

cast light on some of the more enigmatic features of what had happened. By contrast it could scarcely serve to increase the faint element of mystery surrounding his own behaviour.

He was obviously anxious on his wife's part and wanted to have a frank discussion with Rosa, as he might with a surgeon who had operated on her. Quite possibly he wanted reassurance about the likely course of events. There were all sorts of reasons for his wanting to come and see her and his visit could only help to clear the air. So ran her thoughts as she made her way to court and a further round in Terry's contest with authority.

The fact that she got him off with a relatively small fine did nothing to diminish her mood of optimism.

'Thanks, Miss Epton,' he said afterwards, 'you were great. Let me know if you want any stuff for Christmas, I can probably get it for you cheap. Turkeys, a case of scotch, you know the sort of thing?'

Rose did very well, as she shook hands with him and went to her car. Terry invariably offered her largesse of one kind or another after a case, but she always politely refused. There were enough risks in life without accepting Terry's cut-price offerings.

She was back in her office shortly after two o'clock and spent the next hour-and-a-half dictating briefs to counsel.

At three-thirty her phone buzzed and Stephanie announced that Mr Atkins had arrived. A minute later he was ushered in.

He was wearing a brown tweed jacket with suede patches on the elbows, a pair of darker brown slacks and a paisley patterned pullover with a high neckline that hid most of his tie.

'I am sorry I am not properly dressed for a visit to a lawyer,' he said with a small self-deprecating smile. 'But I came straight from the school and didn't go home to change my clothes.'

Rosa could think of the reason for this, but nevertheless asked the question, 'Is your wife still unaware of your coming?'

He nodded slowly. 'I did not wish to worry her,' he said in his precise way, as if words were fragile things which could become easily broken.

'Before we go any further, Mr Atkins, I ought to remind you that it's your wife who is my client and to whom I owe a

65

professional duty. That said, perhaps you'd better now tell me the reason for your visit.'

For a while he sat staring at her as if she were a computer and he was uncertain which button to push first. Then he took a deep breath and said, 'Just how important is my evidence, Miss Epton?'

Whatever Rosa had been expecting, it was certainly not that question and it was her turn to stare back at him.

'It's certainly important,' she said in a puzzled tone, 'because you corroborate your wife's evidence about there being no lights on Jonathan Cool's car and that's going to be the vital issue.' She gave him a wry smile. 'Even though courts rather expect husbands and wives to support one another's stories and, to that extent, tend not to give as much weight to their evidence as to that of an entirely independent witness, it's still important.' She paused and went on, 'Let me put it in a different perspective. As everybody knows you were in the car at the time of the accident it would look extremely odd if you failed to give evidence on your wife's behalf and there was no explanation forthcoming. The jury would be bound to speculate in a way that could only harm your wife's cause. In fact your unexplained failure to appear in the witness box would be most damaging. Does that answer your question?'

'Yes,' he said bleakly and looked away.

'May I ask what prompted it?'

He took another deep breath. 'I've got myself into a foolish position, Miss Epton,' he said giving Rosa a rueful look. 'You see, I was asleep at the time. I had had a bit too much to drink and dozed off on the way home. I woke up as soon as it happened, of course, but I don't actually remember anything beforehand.'

Rosa stared at him in bewilderment. 'Did your wife realise you were asleep?'

'No. I probably wasn't for more than a minute or two.'

'And you've not told her?'

'No. You see, if you were to say my evidence was not so important, I might get out of having to tell her. I would do anything I could to save her further distress.'

'Let me get this absolutely clear, Mr Atkins, are you telling me that you didn't notice Jonathan Cool's car before the accident because you were asleep?'

'I'm afraid that's so.'

'You can't therefore say whether it had any lights on or not?'

'If Sarah says it didn't have any lights, then it can't have had.'

'But you're unable to say that of your own knowledge?'

'I'm afraid that's right.'

'So you made a false statement to the police, as well as to me when you and your wife were here together?'

He nodded. 'I had to stand by Sarah. She was so upset by it all.'

'She's going to be even more so when you tell her what you've just told me.'

He hung his head and looked utterly miserable.

'I wouldn't have had this happen for anything,' he said in an anguished whisper.

'You're going to have to tell her, of course.' He gave a hopeless shrug and Rosa went on, 'On reflection, it'll still be necessary to call you as a witness.'

His head shot up and he stared at her in sudden deep suspicion.

'How can I? I have no evidence to give. . . I've explained.'

'You were a passenger in your wife's car and the worst possible conclusion will be drawn if you don't go into the witness box, if only to explain you were asleep at the time.'

He got up abruptly and sat down again equally suddenly. For a while he held his head in his hands while Rosa observed him with a puzzled expression. Far from clearing the air, the interview had had the opposite effect.

'I do strongly advise you to tell your wife everything when you get home this evening,' she said at length. 'Further postponement can only make things more difficult.'

He gave her an abstracted nod, then in a tentative voice said, 'If Sarah pleaded guilty, would I still have to give evidence?'

Rosa looked at him aghast. 'But your wife has a good defence to the major charge, and there's no question of her being advised

67

to plead guilty. Morever, I'm sure you wouldn't wish her to do so just to save you possible embarrassment in the witness box.'

'It might still be best,' he murmured, almost to himself.

'If your wife wants to plead guilty, it will be entirely against my advice. She's certainly given no indication that she wishes to capitulate. Quite frankly, Mr Atkins, I don't know what to make of your visit. I suggest you go home and have a long talk with your wife, telling her everything you've told me. After which we can have another meeting; the three of us, that is.'

Rosa accompanied him to the door where they gravely shook hands. A few minutes later she went along to her partner's room. Robin Snaith gave her an amused smile as she entered.

'You have that pregnant look,' he remarked.

'I'm totally bewildered, Robin. Listen to this and tell me what you make of it,' Rosa said as she flopped in his visitor's chair.

When she had finished, he said, 'I suppose it just about makes sense and one can rationalise his behaviour. He was loath to tell his wife that he was asleep at the crucial moment and the longer he left it the harder it became. Particularly if she's the trouser-wearing partner.

'But she's not. And anyway I don't believe he did drop off.'

'Why on earth should he say so if it's not true?'

'Because he doesn't want to give evidence. Don't ask me why not because I've no idea. But of one thing I'm absolutely certain, he doesn't want to go anywhere near a court. For some reason he's back-tracking like mad.'

'Out of spite towards his wife, do you think?'

'No, I'm sure it's not that. I believe there's something in his past of which she's totally unaware.'

'Why should an appearance in court bring it to light?'

'It probably wouldn't, but he's afraid that it will. Do you remember my telling you after I'd met him for the first time that there was a slight air of mystery about him?'

'Yes, I do remember. But I can't believe his wife wouldn't also be aware of it. Wouldn't, in fact, know its cause. Wives invariably do.'

'Not always. What about that woman you defended on a forged

prescription charge? She had no idea that her husband was a reprieved murderer who'd spent twelve years in prison.'

'True. And I've always wished that chance hadn't let her find out.' He paused. 'So you think Peter Atkins may have a secret of that sort to hide?'

Rosa nodded. 'I can't think of any other explanation for his strange behaviour.'

'What are you proposing to do about it?'

'I'll phone Mrs Atkins in the morning. That'll tell me soon enough whether he's come clean.'

'And if he hasn't?'

'If he hasn't, I shall come and talk to you again, Robin,' she said with a grin. Then, more seriously, she added, 'It's unusual for a motoring case to throw up so many puzzling features of a human sort. At least it's a change from road measurements and disputed skid marks.'

'I wonder if the identity of the victim has anything to do with it,' Robin said in a contemplative tone. 'Supposing it had just been plain John Smith, local nonentity, and not Jonathan Cool?'

'Now, there's something that hadn't occurred to me,' Rosa remarked as she got up. 'I might try and find out if there's any connection between Peter Atkins and the Cool family.'

'Except that it's not part of your job to probe Peter Atkins's motives. After all, he's not your client.'

'No, but he's come and opened his Pandora's box on my desk. . . I suppose,' she went on in a thoughtful tone, 'that he could always be subpoenaed, though it would be an unusual way to get a husband to court to give evidence on behalf of his wife.'

'I've never known you deterred by the prospect of having to do something unusual,' Robin remarked drily.

Rosa laughed. 'I'd feel much happer if I knew why he's behaving as he is. My instinct tells me he's very much in love with his wife, so why. . . why?'

Chapter 9

On the afternoon that Peter Atkins visited Rosa, he had persuaded his wife to go and see a friend who lived on a farm between Worthing and Horsham and who had a son the same age as Nicole.

He told Sarah that he would be going to London as soon as he finished work around midday (it was his free afternoon) and proposed to visit his friend Geoffrey who was in bed with a back injury. He had shown her Geoffrey's letter received the day before in which he implored Peter to pay him a visit as he was bored stiff. The letter had concluded 'We might even be able to take our current game a few moves further.'

Sarah had never met Geoffrey Traill, though she had often spoken to him on the phone when he always sounded friendly and charming. It had become something of a joke that they had not yet managed to meet face to face. When she and Peter were first married there had been several occasions when a visit by Geoffrey had been arranged, but each time something had intervened to thwart their plans. Once Geoffrey's mother had been taken suddenly ill and he had had to dash up to Yorkshire to see her. On another his firm had sent him abroad at short notice to solve some crisis at their Brussels office and on yet another, when he had been saying third time lucky, his car had broken down and it had taken him several hours to organise its recovery and get himself back to London by train.

Peter had known him for several years before meeting Sarah and they had kept in touch, their friendship fortified by a common interest in chess, hence the concluding sentence of his letter. They had been playing a long-distance game for over a year. Peter would make his moves quite rapidly on the board that was kept on a small table in a corner of the living room. But weeks would go by before Geoffrey sent news of his own next move.

On the day in question, Sarah and Nicole arrived home about six o'clock and Peter came in about an hour-and-a-half later.

'How was your day with Maggie, my darling?' he enquired as he embraced her in the kitchen where she was preparing supper.

'Very enjoyable,' Sarah said with a relaxed smile. 'Nicole and Ben get on so well that Maggie and I were able to have a good old uninterrupted gossip. And how did you find Geoffrey?'

'Feeling sorry for himself, but pleased to see me.'

'How did he hurt his back?'

'Lifting a heavy box off the top of a cupboard.'

'He should be more careful.'

'That's what I told him. He sent you his love.'

'Love from a man I've never met,' Sarah said with a small laugh. 'I suppose we shall meet one day.'

'Of course you will. Trouble at the moment is that he's travelling more than usual, which means he likes to stay at home at weekends.'

'Who's looking after him while he's in bed?'

'A neighbour takes him in food on a tray, but otherwise he can manage. He hopes to be back at work in a few days. The pills he's taking seem to be working.'

While they had been talking, Peter had laid the table in the kitchen alcove. It was like old times with Sarah more relaxed than she had been since the accident, so that he shrank from destroying the atmosphere. At one point on his way home he made up his mind to tell her of his visit to Rosa, making it seem that he had called at her office on the spur of the moment after visiting Geoffrey. He had, in fact, spoken to Geoffrey on the telephone after leaving Rosa, but had not visited him.

Now, however, as he went upstairs to have a wash before supper and to take a peep at his sleeping daughter he realised

71

that further postponement of his news was inevitable. It was unthinkable that he should do anything to spoil Sarah's lighter mood. He would open a bottle of wine when he returned downstairs and later he would make love with all the desperate yearning he felt for her.

The next morning Sarah still seemed relatively relaxed and they decided that they would travel into town together, Peter to Mr Jameson's and mother and daughter in search of a pair of fluffy bedroom slippers for Nicole. After locking the front door they set off down the short garden path swinging a happy Nicole between them. Suddenly a head and shoulders appeared over the top of the hedge, a camera was pointed in their direction and a flashlight exploded.

Nicole was too startled to protest as her father let go of her hand and shot out of the gate.

A small, wiry man wearing a fawn garberdine motoring coat and a check cap was hurrying towards a car which was parked about thirty yards down the road. He had just reached it when Peter caught up with him. There followed a short scuffle which ended with the man falling unceremoniously to the ground, and Peter seizing his camera and opening the back to expose the film.

'Scum,' he hissed at the figure on the ground, as he dropped the camera beside him.

'You won't get away with this,' the man shouted back furiously. 'I'll take you to court for assault and malicious damage. You can join your precious wife in the dock.' As he spoke, he scrambled to his feet and brushed himself down.

For a few seconds they stood glaring at one another, then the man turned and got into his car.

Peter returned to his front gate where Sarah was waiting with an agitated expression.

'You shouldn't have done that, Peter,' she said in an anxious voice.

'Scum,' Peter said angrily. 'That's what he was, just scum.'

'I recognised him,' Sarah murmured. 'I saw him at court the other day. He was talking to Sergeant Hibbert.'

Peter looked at her with a frown.

72

'I can't stop him going to court, but I can stop him taking photographs at my home,' he said after a pause.

'He's not a proper photographer,' Sarah said dully. 'He's Mr Peterson, Cheryl Peterson's father.'

Chapter 10

Joan Peterson was washing up the breakfast things when she heard a car door being slammed with more than usual vigour. A moment later a key was turned in the front door and she glanced over her shoulder into the hall.

'Forget something did you, dear?' she called out to her husband.

Her expression became an anxious frown as Stan came into the kitchen. He had a dishevelled appearance and there were smears of dirt on the front of his gaberdine coat.

'What's happened, Stan?' she asked in a worried voice.

'I've been attacked, that's what's happened,' he said furiously. 'Attacked by the husband of the woman who killed Jonathan. He also broke my camera. I'm going to take out a summons against him for assault and malicious damage. And I'll sue him too.'

'Sit down and tell me what happened,' his wife said in a pacifying tone. 'I'll make you a cup of coffee.'

'I'll go and change first,' he said in a tone of smouldering anger. 'My suit will have to be repaired. There's a tear in the right knee. I'll sue him for that as well.'

When he reappeared five minutes later a cup of coffee was waiting for him on the kitchen table and his wife had completed the washing-up and was drying her hands.

'The bloody man just flew at me and knocked me to the ground,' he said, as Joan hovered beside him.

'But why, Stan? I mean, what were you doing?'

'I wasn't doing anything I hadn't a right to do. I was on a public footpath taking a photograph.'

'A photograph? What of?'

'Of the woman who murdered Jonathan,' he said viciously.

'But where?'

'At their home. The two of them with their child were coming down their path and I took a photograph of them over the top of the hedge.'

Joan frowned. 'Why on earth did you want to do that, Stan?'

'Why shouldn't I?' he demanded resentfully. 'It's still a so-called free country.'

'But why photograph the Atkinses at all?'

'Because she's still walking around as if she's done nothing wrong. Just wait till a judge and jury have put her where she belongs!'

His wife sighed. Stan had never been a relaxed and easy-going sort of person, but since Jonathan's death he had become obsessed with seeing justice done, as he called it. The tragedy seemed to prey on his mind even more than on Cheryl's. She was still upset and bitter, but her father was positively vindictive in his attitude. Hardly an evening passed without his rehearsing Cheryl in her evidence and instructing her how to face cross-examination.

'I wouldn't do anything hasty, dear,' his wife said peaceably.

'Nothing's going to stop me taking out a summons against him.'

'Won't it look as if you're conducting a personal vendetta?'

'What! After he's assaulted me in the street!'

Joan sighed again. 'But it'll come out that you were photographing his wife in their garden and surely the court would want to know why. You'd have to explain that, wouldn't you, dear?'

'I wasn't doing anything wrong,' he said defiantly.

'Of course you weren't, but why *were* you taking the photograph?'

'I was going to sell it to a newspaper,' he said in a grudging voice.

His wife nodded thoughtfully. She suspected that the profit motive was combined with that of wanting to harass the unfortunate woman. Not that Stan would ever admit it.

'It wouldn't sound very good in court, would it?'

'Why not?'

'And it might be used against Cheryl when she gives her evidence.' She paused. 'And we wouldn't want that to happen, would we?'

He drank what was left of his coffee and pushed the cup and saucer towards his wife who picked them up and carried them over to the sink.

'I suppose you may have a point,' he said in an ungracious tone. 'But Mr bloody Atkins needn't think he's going to get away with it, because he's not. I'll get my own back somehow.'

'Did anyone see what happened?'

He gave an impatient shrug. 'I've no idea. There was somebody about a hundred yards further along the road, but he was walking away from us. I don't know if any of the neighbours were looking out of a window. They're a stuck-up lot in that road. Think they're superior because they're close to the golf course and away from all the day trippers.'

Joan was relieved on all counts that there hadn't apparently been any independent witnesses, for if somebody had come forward to support Stan it would have fortified him in his determination to take action and if it had been somebody on the Atkinses' side it would make Stan's extrication from the affair that much more difficult. She was now reasonably confident that he wouldn't take the matter any further. He would continue to huff and puff, but he wouldn't go dashing off to court and applying for a summons against his attacker.

He pushed his chair back and got up. 'Phone June at the office and tell her I've been held up,' he said as he turned to leave the kitchen.

June was the telephonist at Henner & Co. She was an amiable girl, but not very good at her job, her forte being to cut people off in mid-conversation and them blame the antiquated switchboard over which she presided.

Joan waved until Stan had driven off before going to the phone.

'That you, June, dear? It's Joan Peterson. I'm afraid Stan'll be a bit late this morning. He's on his way now, but he got held up.'

'Mr Peter Henner was asking for him just now and seemed a bit cross he wasn't in. He's all right, is he?'

'Yes, he's perfectly all right.'

'How's Cheryl?'

'Still very upset as you'd expect and not looking forward to the ordeal of giving evidence.'

'It'll be a big moment for her,' June observed, as though it might be the final round of a beauty competition. 'I'd love to have met Jonathan Cool.'

'He was charming and we all miss him terribly.'

'I bet. Wouldn't it have been wonderful to have had him as a son-in-law?'

Whatever Joan Peterson's thoughts on this subject, she was not prepared to divulge them to the telephonist at Henner & Co. Saying that she was sure June must be very busy, she said goodbye and rang off. As she did so, her eye lit upon her husband's camera which was on the hall table.

Stan had always been a keen photographer and fancied himself as a near professional. She picked the camera up and examined it. There was a small piece of grass stuck to the lens and some traces of mud on the back, otherwise it appeared to be undamaged. She now recalled having seen Stan put in a new film only the previous day, presumably in readiness for his candid camera foray.

She wished the trial could be over and done with as quickly as possible. The wait was having its effect on both Cheryl and Stan. She herself felt less emotionally involved. She bore Sarah no personal ill-will, though she didn't doubt her daughter's version of what happened.

The Atkinses obviously had money or they could not have afforded the sort of house in which they lived. He couldn't be all that well paid as a teacher at Mr Jameson's, so presumably one of them had private means.

It was with these vague and inconclusive thoughts passing through her mind that she went upstairs to make the beds.

Chapter 11

Peter and Sarah drove into town in grim silence, leaving Nicole to prattle away to herself in the back of the car without parental interruption.

Peter sat tight-lipped beside his wife who was driving as she normally did when they were out together. Though not for much longer, she reflected unhappily, with certain disqualification facing her for the breathalyser offence.

She was still shaken by his aggressive reaction to the man with the camera (she had no doubt it was Cheryl's father) and alarmed at what the consequences might be. It was so out of character for Peter to behave like that – or would have been until a few weeks ago. There was no disputing the fact that Peter had changed since the accident. But he had shown no inclination to admit it or even talk about it. The effect on Sarah had been to increase her general misery and fill her with a sense of foreboding.

As she drew up outside Mr Jameson's he leaned over to kiss her.

'See you this evening, my darling.' Turning round in his seat he blew Nicole a kiss.

After he had got out of the car and given his wife and daughter a final wave, Sarah drove off and parked at a meter in the centre of town. Nicole was a remarkably sturdy walker for her age so Sarah left her push-chair in the boot. Having purchased the bedroom slippers, Nicole wanted to go down to the sea front to see the waves. Waves was one of the first words she had learnt and watching them break on the beach in a surge of foam had always been a source of endless fascination to her.

They were just walking past a café in a street that led to the promenade when Sarah heard a brisk tapping on glass. She looked round and saw Mr Jameson sitting by himself at a table in the café window. He beckoned them to come in and join him.

Nicole's face lit up when Sarah drew her attention to him. They had always enjoyed the sort of rapport often found between the very young and the very old.

By the time they got inside Mr Jameson had drawn up two more chairs.

'Fancy seeing you here, Jamie!' Sarah said, as Nicole planted a kiss on his pickled cheek. Despite their rapport she was averse to being kissed by him on account of his moustache.

'I had to visit the bank manager,' he said, 'and thought I'd have a little light refreshment before I went back.'

Sarah smiled as she glanced at the half-eaten chocolate éclair in front of him. He had a weakness for cream cakes and even on occasions secreted them in one of his desk drawers.

'What would you and Nicole like?' he asked when a lady in a flowered smock came to take their order.

'I'll have a cup of coffee,' Sarah said, 'Nicole would love a coke.'

Nicole's attention had become focused on a small boy who was standing in a doorway at the rear of the café. He was observing her with equal interest.

'There's my grandson, Ian,' the lady in the smock said, 'would you like to come and meet him?'

Nicole nodded solemnly and clambered off her chair.

'She gets on well with other children,' Sarah remarked as she toddled away, 'she really ought to have a brother or sister of her own.'

'Perhaps one day she will have,' Mr Jameson said.

'I'm getting a bit too old for babies, Jamie.'

'Nonsense. You're only in your early thirties.'

'Peter will be forty-five next birthday.'

'That puts you both in the prime of life.'

Sarah decided it was time to change the subject. 'Did you walk into town?' she asked.

'No. My bicycle's parked round the corner. Chained to some

railings. A few years ago I'd never have dreamt of putting on chains and padlocks every time I left it. We just used to prop our bikes against the kerb and they'd still be there when we returned. The world may be a better place in many ways since I was young, but not as regards everyday honesty.'

'As I feel at the moment, Jamie, nothing's better than it used to be.'

'Has something happened to depress you? Something on top of everything else, I mean?'

'Did you see Peter this morning?' she asked by way of reply.

'Yes.'

'Did he tell you about a man trying to take photographs as we left the house?'

'No. We spoke only briefly and that was on the subject of a new timetable. Why, what happened?'

Sarah told him while he ate the rest of his éclair.

'And you believe this man was Miss Peterson's father?' he said when she had finished.

'I'm certain of it.'

'Whether or not he was within his rights, it was most reprehensible of him. An invasion of privacy, isn't that the fashionable cry these days?'

'But Peter shouldn't have reacted as he did.'

'He was just being over-protective. Seeing you harassed in that way made him angry.'

'It was more than that, Jamie. I'm sure of it. He's been behaving strangely ever since the accident. You've had evidence of it yourself.'

Mr Jameson blew through his moustache and looked thoughtful.

'Your husband's obviously a very complex person,' he remarked slowly. 'We're all complex creatures, of course, but some more so than others. I know he had an unhappy childhood, brought up in an institution and all that, and it's clearly left its mark. Incidentally, does he ever talk about those early days?'

She shook her head. 'He's told me he prefers not to remember them and that's been that.'

80

'Does he have any relatives?'

'No.'

'No brothers or sisters or cousins?'

'None that he's ever mentioned.'

'Would I be correct in thinking that you don't know a great deal about his background?'

'Practically nothing. I've always respected his reticence and I've never asked him what you might call awkward questions. As you know, Jamie, we fell in love with one another almost immediately and our love has been sufficient to sustain us until. . . It still does sustain us,' she added vehemently.

'Of course, and will, I'm sure, continue to do so. Every marriage goes through the furnace at some stage or another and usually emerges stronger.'

She gave him a quizzical look. 'Do you really believe that, Jamie?'

'Certainly I do. And there's no doubt in my mind that Peter's still deeply in love with you.'

'I want to believe that, but sometimes of late I've wondered. It's not that he doesn't show me as much affection as before, but it's the deception that seems to have crept in. That curious business when Cecily Young saw him at Worthing station. When I asked him about it, he gave me an explanation, but I'm certain it wasn't the truth. And then his not wanting to come to court with me and those mysterious phone calls from public boxes. And his assault on Mr Peterson this morning.' She paused. 'What's it all add up to, Jamie?'

Mr Jameson wished he knew the answer. Meanwhile, however, there was one line of enquiry he had decided to follow up.

'There is one person I might approach,' Sarah went on. 'He's Peter's closest friend, though oddly enough I've never met him. His name's Geoffrey Traill and Peter went up to London yesterday to visit him. He's confined to his bed with a bad back. It's possible that Peter has confided in him and, if I play my cards right, he might be able to tell me something which will put my mind at rest. That's all I'm seeking, Jamie, reassurance.' She looked thoughtful. 'I wish I'd met Geoffrey, that would make it

81

much simpler. He always sounds very friendly on the phone, but it won't be easy broaching the subject with somebody who is only a voice. Particularly as I shall have to ask him not to tell Peter that I've spoken to him.' She gave Mr Jameson a rueful smile. 'That's the awful thing about deception, it breeds more deception.'

Chapter 12

Mr Jameson put on his bicycle-clips and mounted the ancient bike that had carried him tens of thousands of miles.

It was a cold day and he was wearing the thickest of his black jackets, which, apart from a shiny waterproof cape for rainy days, was his maximum protection against the elements.

The wind was against him, but he found it exhilarating as he pedalled steadily on his way. He was glad of his fortuitous encounter with Sarah, even though it had given him much to think about. She was right, of course, about Peter, he was a changed person. Nothing dramatic, but changed for all that.

As soon as he got back to the school and had locked his cycle away in its shed, he went to his study and pulled out a large box file in which he kept all correspondence relating to staff. It didn't take him long to find the two letters for which he was looking.

The first was dated 18th February 1979 and came from Mr Howard Pearson, manager of the Baker Street branch of the Southern Counties Bank.

Dear Sir (wrote Mr Pearson),

In answer to your letter concerning Mr Peter Atkins, I am pleased to give the reference you seek. I have known Mr Atkins for five years and, in my view, he is most suitable for the appointment under consideration. He is intelligent, hard-working and reliable. He is also a person of great charm who should have no difficulty getting on with his colleagues and the students of your school. Additionally he possesses great patience, which, I imagine, is an asset in the

teaching profession. I endorse his candidature most warmly.
Yours truly
Howard Pearson.

The second letter was dated 24th February 1979 and was from Miss Bridget Duxbury of 119 Sudmore Road, London N22, who wrote:

Dear Mr Jameson,
I am delighted to give Peter Atkins my sincerest recommendation. I am a retired schoolmistress and have known him for several years. I can think of nobody better suited to fill the post you refer to in your letter, as, in my view, he has all the necessary qualifications – patience, reliability and conscientiousness, not to mention intelligence and a capacity for hard work. He is also a charming person.
I often used to visit Worthing as a child and your letter brought back many memories of the place.
With best wishes to you and to your school.
Yours sincerely
Bridget Duxbury

As Mr Jameson put the letter down he recalled that Miss Duxbury had phoned him in a fluster because she believed she had wrongly addressed her letter and he mightn't receive it. He was able to tell her it had already arrived.
As a result of these two references and his own impression of Peter Atkins he had had no hesitation in offering him the job. Nor had he ever regretted doing so. He still had no regrets, even if the time seemed to have come when he should make a few discreet enquiries to allay the vague doubts that had begun to trouble him.
Both letters had telephone numbers and he decided to start off by calling Miss Duxbury, having already once talked to her. When he dialled her number, however, there was a total silence. With some difficulty he managed to get through to the exchange who told him that the number he wanted was unallocated and

they couldn't help him further. After a further ten frustrating minutes he was informed that there was no such London subscriber as Bridget Duxbury. He was forced to assume, therefore, that she had either moved elsewhere, or possibly even died.

He would certainly have accepted one of these assumptions had he not been equally balked in his attempt to phone the Baker Street branch of the Southern Counties Bank. It took him three calls to discover that the branch in question had closed two years previously and that its manager in February 1979 was not a Mr Howard Pearson.

Though he accepted coincidences as a fact of life, this was too much for him to take without further enquiry. Accordingly the next day he donned his best clothes for a visit to London, gave his battered black homburg a bit of a brush and set off without telling anyone where he was going. In his wallet were the two letters he had received from Peter Atkins's referees.

When he reached Victoria Station he took a taxi to the head branch of the Southern Counties Bank in the city. It was smaller than he had expected and seemed overshadowed by other vast financial institutions around it. He entered with a confident step and found it deserted. Maybe the head office didn't do anything as vulgar as hand money over a counter. He approached a young clerk who was eyeing him and produced Mr Pearson's letter.

'I should like to speak to somebody about this letter,' he said. 'I telephoned yesterday and was told your Baker Street branch had been closed. However, I'd like to get in touch with Mr Howard Pearson, who signed this letter.'

'Just take a seat, sir, and I'll see what I can find out.'

Mr Jameson went and sat down on a chair in a corner and looked around him.

How they loved marble when they built these temples to finance, he reflected.

There was a copy of *The Financial Times* on the table beside him and he picked it up. He had barely done so when the young clerk re-appeared and Mr Jameson went over to where he stood behind a sheet of bulletproof glass.

'Mr Appleton will be with you shortly, sir,' the clerk said.

'What is Mr Appleton's position in the bank?'

'He's an assistant manager.'

At that moment a door opened in what appeared to be a solid marble wall and a man with rimless spectacles and a near-military haircut called out Mr Jameson's name.

The two men shook hands and Mr Appleton stood aside and ushered Mr Jameson into a small but tastefully appointed interview room. He had Mr Pearson's letter in his hand and laid it on the desk between them as he sat down.

'I'm afraid you've had rather a wasted journey,' he said. 'I'm sorry you weren't put through to me when you rang yesterday as I might have been able to save you coming.'

'But surely there's an explanation,' Mr Jameson said, pointing at the letter. 'No such branch: no such manager!'

Mr Appleton gave him a small, wintry smile.

'The branch existed. But it was one of our few sites which wasn't freehold and when the lease expired we decided to close it. The nearest branch is now in Queensway.'

'And Mr Howard Pearson, what about him?'

Mr Appleton frowned as he might have if his arm were jogged when lifting a cup of coffee to his lips.

'At the date this letter was sent,' he went on, 'the manager of our Baker Street branch was Mr Arthur Milling. Unhappily he was away sick for the first part of the year and died shortly after an early retirement on health grounds.'

Mr Jameson was not disposed to waste time or sympathy on Mr Milling's fate.

'So where does Mr Howard Pearson come into the picture?' he persisted.

'I'm afraid that's a question I can't answer,' Mr Appleton replied frostily.

Can't or won't, Mr Jameson wanted to say, but refrained.

'Was there anyone of that name at your Baker Street branch?' he enquired with a trace of impatience. 'After all, this letter was sent in answer to one I'd addressed to a Mr Howard Pearson.'

'I can't tell you. It would mean searching through files of staff records.'

'I find to hard to believe that you couldn't turn up the answer in a matter of seconds. I thought banks with all their computers were in the vanguard of business efficiency.'

'Perhaps you'd care to tell me why you're so interested in tracing this Mr Pearson three years after he wrote to you?' Mr Appleton riposted in a steely voice. 'Presumably the reference he gave was perfectly satisfactory at the time?'

'That's beside the point,' Mr Jameson said belligerently. 'The fact remains that it was an apparent forgery emanating from your bank.'

Mr Appleton gave his visitor a cold stare. Then he shrugged and said, 'I'm sorry we're unable to help you, Mr Jameson, but three years is a long time in the life of a busy bank. Staff come and go and people's recollection fades.' He picked the letter up from the table. 'I imagine you wish to hold on to this?'

'Aren't you even sufficiently interested to want a copy?'

'I've already taken the liberty of making one.'

It was just on midday when Mr Jameson emerged from the bank, baffled and frustrated. He found a sandwich bar along the street and pushed his way inside. Oblivious of the curious glances he attracted, he perched himself uncomfortably on the only free stool and ordered a cup of coffee and a cheese and tomato sandwich.

The prospect of making his way to N.22 in the hope of tracing Miss Duxbury depressed him, but failed to lessen his determination. He had always regarded North London as a suburban wilderness best seen, if at all, through the window of a speeding train.

He dived into the underground and, after one change, alighted at Wood Green. A policeman on the pavement outside the station gave him directions to Sudmore Road. About a fifteen-minute walk, he informed Mr Jameson with a carefully appraising look.

He was already feeling tired by the time he reached Sudmore Road and his heart sank when he saw its length. It was dead straight and had small Victorian villas on either side. The odd numbers were on the further side and he crossed over and began his trek with the resolve of an explorer. From time to time he would glance at a front door to see how much farther he had to go. It seemed an age before he reached number 101. Only ten more before he came to 119. He peered ahead and reckoned it must be next to a shop on a corner. As he got closer he could see it was a small general-store-cum-sub-post-office. There was a letter box on the pavement outside. He walked past it and stopped at the gate of the neighbouring house. '121', he read.

There was nothing for it but to go into the shop and enquire. An agreeable, spicy smell assailed his nose as he entered. There was a young Indian at a cash desk near the door and an older man, also from the Indian subcontinent, behind a grille at the post office end of the premises.

Mr Jameson addressed himself to the young man at the cash desk.

'Can you tell me please which is number 119?'

The young man gave him a slow smile. 'It is here,' he said.

'You mean, this is 119 Sudmore Road?'

'Yes.'

'Oh!'

The young man lowered his gaze to the magazine that lay beside the till. Mr Jameson noticed that it was open at an article entitled 'Philosophical Reflections'.

'I was looking for a Miss Duxbury who used to live at this number,' Mr Jameson went on hopefully.

The young man looked up and shook his head. 'Not now.'

'Do you know where I can find her?'

'Perhaps my father can help you,' he said, indicating the older man behind the grille, who had greying hair and a fierce moustache.

Mr Jameson walked towards him.

'Good afternoon, I wonder if you can help me. . .'

'Good afternoon to you, sir,' the man said graciously. 'I hear what you ask my son, but no Miss Duxbury lives here, I'm afraid.'

'But you know the name?'

'No, sir, I did not mean to give that impression. To tell you the absolute truth, I have never heard of Miss Duxbury.'

'May I ask how long you've been here?'

'Two years next 31st March.'

'Perhaps Miss Duxbury lived here before you came?' Mr Jameson glanced up at the ceiling. 'I take it there's living accommodation above?'

'Indeed there is, sir, but Miss Duxbury did not live there. I bought the business from Mr Jablonski and he and his wife had been here for fifteen years. Maybe before them. . .'

Mr Jameson shook his head in a bemused fashion. After a pause, during which somebody came in and bought a single stamp, he said, 'It's very strange. I had a letter from Miss Duxbury about three years ago giving this address. Moreover it was a reply to one I had sent her here.'

'Most strange, sir,' the Indian agreed.

'May I enquire what your telephone number is?'

'We have one number for here and one for our flat upstairs.'

'Is either of them this number?' Mr Jameson asked, showing him the letter-head of Miss Duxbury's letter.

'No, sir. Neither of our numbers is that one.'

'Have you any idea how I might get in touch with Mr Jablonski?'

'Unhappily, Mr and Mrs Jablonski were divorcing, that is why they wished to sell the business. Mrs Jablonski went off with her lover and Mr Jablonski went to live with his married daughter in Canada. He was Polish, but couldn't go back to his native country.' As if in answer to Mr Jameson's unspoken question, he added, 'I do not have the address of either Mr or Mrs Jablonski. It is a pity that I cannot help you, sir.'

Mr Jameson gave him a tired smile. 'I'm sorry, too,' he said, 'but you've been most kind.'

As he trudged back along Sudmore Road, which seemed to have grown in length, he felt thwarted and exhausted. He had left home that morning in a spirit of adventure, but was returning defeated. Instead of laying ghosts, he had created fresh ones. And yet there must be a simple explanation for what appeared to be

89

two fake references.

It was not until he was on the train back to Worthing that he decided what to do next. He would speak to Rosa Epton and put it all in her lap. For the time being he wouldn't say anything to Peter himself, nor to Sarah, whose anxieties could only be increased by what he had found out.

It had been a long day for someone of his age and he had seldom felt so uncertain and dispirited.

Chapter 13

Rosa had not, as she'd originally intended, phoned Sarah the day after Peter Atkins's visit to her office. She had decided on reflection that it would be better to let the initiative come from the other side. There was no pressing need for her to get in touch with Sarah, though she would probably do so within the next four or five days. The fact that Sarah didn't try and get in touch with her was evidence enough that her husband had not yet broached the subject of his evidence.

In any event Rosa found herself heavily occupied with another case over the next two days. The daughter of a wealthy businessman had been arrested at Heathrow and charged with possessing forged travellers' cheques, and Rosa had been required to attend court at short notice and later arrange for a bail application before a High Court judge in chambers. The girl's father had virtually stood over Rosa every stage, angrily chafing and threatening to call his M.P. and the editor of a Sunday newspaper who was a close friend. Eventually the girl, Julia Bannerman-Jones, was released on bail, but it had been an exhausting and time-consuming exercise.

When she arrived in the office just after nine o'clock on the morning after all this, it was to be informed by Stephanie that Mr Jameson had already been on the telephone.

'He was there when I plugged in,' Stephanie said in a slightly affronted tone, 'and it wasn't that I was late. I told him to call again about nine-thirty and you'd probably be here.' Just then a light began blinking on the small switchboard. 'I bet that's him now,' she said, 'and it's still only ten past.' She flicked a switch. 'Good morning, Snaith and Epton, can I help you?' She gave

Rosa a long-suffering nod.

'I'll take it in my room,' Rosa said quickly and hurried along the passage.

'I was frightened I'd miss you,' Mr Jameson said breathlessly when he was put through. 'Your telephone girl said not to ring back till nine-thirty, but I thought you might have left for court by then. I'm greatly relieved to hear your voice.'

'What's happened?' Rosa asked.

'I went up to London yesterday and what a day I had. . . I just don't know what to make of it.'

Without further prompting he launched into an account of his visits to the Southern Counties Bank and to 119 Sudmore Road.

'I just don't know what to make of it,' he repeated when at length he finished his recital of events.

'Have you said anything to Peter Atkins?'

'Haven't seen him yet this morning. He's not due in till later. His first class today is at eleven. He's so good at his job too, so why does he have to supply fake references? I mean, they must be false, mustn't they?'

'Sounds very much like it,' Rosa remarked thoughtfully.

'Well, I'm glad to have unburdened myself. I hardly slept a wink last night. I'm so concerned for Sarah. Her whole world seems to be falling apart.'

Rosa pondered. First there had been Peter Atkins's clandestine visit to her office, now Mr Jameson's disclosures. She wished she could make sense of it.

After a pause she said, 'What I mustn't lose sight of is that I'm representing Sarah Atkins on specific motoring charges and her husband's somewhat odd behaviour doesn't really impinge upon the case. It's no more than a peripheral matter.'

'But he's a vital witness,' Mr Jameson exclaimed.

Rosa let this pass. Peter's visit to her was a matter of professional confidence, even though, strictly speaking, he wasn't her client.

'I take it,' she said, 'that you don't intend mentioning any of this to Sarah?'

92

'Certainly not. I have no wish to worry her more than necessary. That's why I decided to lay it all at your door, Rosa. I said to myself, Rosa will know exactly what to do.'

And what do I do? Rosa wondered after Mr Jameson had eventually rung off. She wished Robin was in his office, but knew that he had gone straight to court from home and wouldn't be in till late afternoon, so she couldn't run along the passage and consult him.

She was still pondering when her phone buzzed and Stephanie announced that Mrs Atkins was on the line.

'Is that you, Rosa? It is all right to call you Rosa, isn't it?'

'Please do.'

'And I'm Sarah, as you know,' she went on breathlessly. 'I'm coming up to London today. Would it be possible to come in and see you?'

'When would suit you?'

'Is three o'clock convenient?'

'Fine. I was going to call you anyway.'

'Has something further happened?' she enquired anxiously.

'I've now heard that the D.P.P. have definitely taken over the case. Also I have a copy of the prosecution statements which we can go through together. And I'm afraid the analyst to whom I sent the blood sample you handed me confirms that you were just over the legal limit.'

'Do the statements contain any unpleasant surprises?'

'Not really. Cheryl Peterson's has a nasty vindictive ring about it. But the more vindictive she is the better our chance of discrediting her evidence.'

Sarah let out a small groan. 'Peter assaulted Mr Peterson two days ago. He was trying to take a photograph of me outside our house. I'll tell you about it this afternoon.'

Their conversation finished, Rosa packed her briefcase ready for court.

'I'll be back at lunchtime, Stephanie,' she announced on her way out. She still had to decide what to say, if anything, about Peter's visit to her office. There was no indication that he had yet

93

broken his news to his wife.

Sarah arrived ten minutes early.

'As I'm going on to see somebody after leaving here, I hoped you wouldn't mind my coming ahead of time,' she said as Rosa met her at the door of her office.

'That's perfectly all right. I'm here and waiting for custom,' Rosa said with a smile.

She had scarcely spoken the words when the phone buzzed and Stephanie said, 'Mr Bannerman-Jones is on the line. I told him you were engaged with a client, but he said it was most urgent to have a quick word with you before he went off to an important meeting.'

'O.K., Stephanie, you'd better put him through.' Placing a hand over the mouthpiece she turned to Sarah and said, 'Sorry about this interruption, but have a look at these statements while I'm on the phone.'

In the event Mr Bannerman-Jones's call was neither brief nor urgent. Fortunately he did all the talking and Rosa only had to contribute the occasional monosyllable.

'I apologise,' she said to Sarah when eventually her caller had rung off.

Sarah glanced up from the file of statements she was holding. She looked tense and upset.

'The girl's statement is a grotesque piece of perjury,' she said in a voice that trembled.

'It's no more than we expected.'

'I suppose not, but somehow seeing it written down and signed seems to make it worse.'

'As I've always said, the case will be a straight contest between your word and hers.'

'My word and Peter's against hers,' Sarah corrected her.

Here was further confirmation that Peter hadn't dropped his bombshell. Rosa felt suddenly exasperated, as well as embarrassed by the position in which he had placed her.

'Yours is the vital evidence,' she said, after a pause. 'I doubt whether a jury will set great store by what Peter says. If they accept your word against Cheryl Peterson's, they'll acquit you regardless of Peter's evidence. But if not, then nothing Peter might say would be likely to tilt the balance in your favour.'

Sarah shivered. 'You put it very clinically.'

'It's my job to be realistic,' Rosa replied. 'If it's any comfort, I happen to believe your version of what happened, even though I don't have to believe in your innocence in order to defend you. Incidentally, there's one point I didn't fully cover when I took your proof of evidence. Were you and Peter talking immediately prior to the accident?'

'Yes. We were discussing the party. Why?'

'I just wondered. You weren't feeling sleepy at all?'

'On the contrary I felt remarkably wide-awake. We were talking most of the time. I think we probably both saw the other car at the same moment. I remember Peter letting out a sort of shout a split second before it happened.'

Rosa nodded and made a brief note on her scribbling pad. So why was Peter Atkins now saying he was asleep when the accident took place? The answer seemed to be clear enough: he didn't want to be drawn into giving evidence on his wife's behalf. But why not? It was the answer to that further question that presented such an enigma.

'How is Peter?' Rosa enquired.

Sarah's expression clouded. 'You obviously realise that I'm worried about him, don't you?'

'Well, yes. I realised you were upset when he didn't come to court that day. And then you mentioned on the phone yesterday that he'd assaulted Cheryl Peterson's father. What exactly happened?'

Sarah described the incident. At the end she let out a sigh. 'I feel I'm living in a dream,' she went on. 'A not at all pleasant dream. I don't want to burden you with all my personal problems, Rosa, but I've reached the point where I live in perpetual dread as to what's going to happen next.'

'Can't you sit down together and have a really frank talk?'

'Peter's never been very good at talking, it's more his nature to keep things bottled up. Even so we were wonderfully happy until

95

this happened. The accident, I mean. Now it's all changed. It's not that he's been unkind to me, let alone shown me any physical violence, it's just that. . . that he's somehow different. As though he's being controlled by some outside force. I know it sounds absurd, but. . .' She left the sentence unfinished.

'Has he talked about the case recently?'

Sarah shook her head. 'For some reason I'm sure he doesn't want to become involved. He'd sooner not give evidence. . .'

'Has he said as much to you?' Rosa broke in.

'No, he wouldn't because he knows how much I'm depending on him. I accept what you said just now about it really being my word against Cheryl Peterson's, but a jury's bound to be impressed by Peter's transparent sincerity and truthfulness.' She paused and gave Rosa a look that pleaded for belief. 'He's been a marvellous husband and he dotes on Nicole.'

'Had he been married before?' Rosa asked.

'No. Why do you ask that?'

'I just wondered. I gather he was over forty when you met. Most men are married by that age, if they're going to be.'

'Peter wasn't.' Her tone was sharp and a second later she apologised. 'I'm sorry, I didn't mean to sound rude.'

Rosa stretched out an arm to answer the telephone that suddenly gave one of its imperious buzzes.

'Yes, hold on,' she said with a slight frown. Passing the receiver to Sarah she added, 'It's for you.'

Sarah looked flustered. 'Who on earth. . . ? Hello, Sarah Atkins speaking. . . . oh, I see. . . . I'm sorry. . . . no, that's perfectly all right, I quite understand. . . . yes, I hope so, too. . . . Thank you for letting me know . . . goodbye.'

She handed the phone back to Rosa, her expression a mixture of resignation and annoyance.

'I'd better explain,' she said. 'I was planning to visit an old friend of Peter's whom I've never met. I thought maybe a talk with him might help to. . . well, might help. I phoned him this morning and arranged to visit him at four-thirty, but that was him on the line saying he can't now make it. He has a sudden urgent business meeting and his office was sending a car to pick

96

him up. He's been at home with a bad back. Peter came up to town to see him a few days ago.'

'Did you tell him you'd be at this number?'

'I merely said I'd be calling on my solicitor before going to see him. Peter must have mentioned your name when *he* went to see him.' She bit her lip nervously. 'I had great difficulty discovering his number as I didn't want Peter to know I was proposing to visit him. Peter had torn up a recent letter from Geoffrey – his name's Geoffrey Traill by the way – but I retrieved the pieces from the refuse bin and managed to put them together. I didn't tell Geoffrey that, of course.'

'Did you say why you wanted to see him?'

'Not exactly. I said I was coming up to London anyway and thought it'd be an opportunity to meet him. I did say that I looked forward to talking to him about Peter as he'd known him longer than I had and I added that, for reasons I'd explain when I saw him, Peter was unaware of my proposed visit. He's always been tremendously friendly when we've spoken on the phone; he did suggest, however, that we should postpone a meeting until he was finally fit again. It was at that stage, I suppose, I sounded a bit desperate and he agreed to my coming. I can't help wondering now if he ever intended we should meet.'

'Where does he live?'

'He has a flat on the north side of Clapham Common.' With a slight note of bitterness she added, 'But perhaps he's a mere figment of Peter's imagination: a piece of fictitious background.' She paused. 'I don't really mean that. It's just that I'm totally bewildered.'

And would be even more so, Rosa reflected, if you knew what Mr Jameson discovered and if I told you that your husband had sat in that same chair a few days ago and said that he couldn't really give any evidence because he'd been asleep and perhaps it would be best if you pleaded guilty.

'Anyway,' Sarah now went on in a depressed voice. 'What's the next thing to happen in my case?'

'The D.P.P. will serve a fresh set of statements on us which'll be substantially the same as the ones you've just read. After that a date will be fixed for the committal proceedings. I think we'll almost certainly be prepared to accept what is called a paper committal. That means the magistrates won't be required to consider the evidence and the committal to the crown court will be a formality. There's no point in fighting at the lower court unless there's a good chance of getting the case thrown out.'

'Why can't we fight it there?' Sarah asked querulously.

'Principally because the statements present a prima facie case and that's all the magistrates have to decide. They're not trying the case. If we did fight it, we couldn't dislodge the prosecution evidence and we should have disclosed our defence to no avail.'

'But my defence has already been disclosed in my statement.'

'I know, but that's different from holding a full dress rehearsal.'

'I'd give anything for it all to be over and done with now. . . tomorrow.'

'I realise how you feel. Waiting is one of the hardest parts and I'm afraid the law isn't renowned for its quickness. The trouble is that most courts have a considerable backlog of cases and people in custody invariably get priority over those on bail. However, once the committal proceedings are over, I'll do everything I can to fix an early date of trial. The D.P.P. is generally quite co-operative in such matters.'

'It seems to me that just because I had the misfortune to knock down someone famous, I'm to face a state trial,' Sarah remarked with a touch of bitterness. 'I mean, the very fact of the Public Prosecutor taking over the case.'

'That's one of his functions. To intervene in cases of special public interest and ensure the sort of impartiality they mightn't receive at a local level.' Rosa paused and went on, 'As your solicitor in the case, it's not my business, but I do suggest you have a good talk with Peter and try and get him to tell you what's troubling him.'

'You don't know him, Rosa. He can shut up tighter than a clam when he wants. All I can do is cross my fingers and hope. . . Hope that I don't end up in prison.'

'That's extremely unlikely, so don't even think about it!'

Sarah reached for her handbag and stood up.

'Will you let me know as soon as you have any further news?'

'Of course. And you get in touch with me if anything happens your end.'

'Such as Mr Peterson throwing a brick through our window perhaps,' Sarah observed sardonically.

'Such as anything untoward at all,' Rosa replied.

Chapter 14

'Where's Cheryl?' Stan Peterson asked when he got home that evening. He threw his wife an accusing look as though she were guilty of spiriting their daughter away. He was still smarting from his treatment at the hands of Peter Atkins, and though he had heeded his wife's advice and not taken out a summons for assault, he was determined to get even in some way.

'She's in her room,' Joan said, looking up from mending one of his socks. 'I wish she'd go away for a few days,' she went on in a worried tone. 'She needs a break, the case has really got her down. She's withdrawn and almost resents being spoken to.'

'Not surprising, is it! She's suffering from delayed shock,' Stan said with an ever prompt answer. 'Going away isn't necessarily the answer. I'll go up and have a talk with her. If she listens to me she's got nothing to worry about. Giving evidence is a piece of cake, as I keep telling her.'

'I just wish she didn't have to be a witness,' Joan said in a resigned tone.

'Well, she does have to be. Apart from anything else she owes it to Jonathan to see that the Atkins woman gets her just deserts. I was talking to Sergeant Hibbert today and said I hoped the D.P.P. would pull out all the stops and really go for her. It's not a case for any pussyfooting.'

'What did he say?'

'He obviously agreed with me even if he didn't actually say so. But he's never been a particularly forthcoming fellow. I'll go up and have a word with Cheryl.'

100

He found his daughter sitting on the bed painting her fingernails.

'I gather from mum you're not feeling too chirpy,' he said, brushing her cheek with the back of his hand.

'I'm all right,' she said, moving her head away.

'You can't fool your dad. I can tell when something's wrong. It's still the thought of giving evidence that's worrying you, isn't it?'

'Look, dad, I just don't want to be reminded of it all the time. Give me a break. I'm sick of all the instruction of how to behave when I'm in court.'

'I've only been going through things for your benefit, Cheryl. After all, I know what I'm talking about. I see witnesses in the box every day. It's all a question of impressing a jury.'

'So you keep on telling me.'

'What's your problem then?'

She shook her head in a gesture of impatience. 'I keep on telling you, I don't want to talk about it, that's all.'

Stan frowned. But a moment later he said, 'Why don't you come downstairs and watch a bit of television before supper? It'll help relax you. I'll open a bottle of that rosé wine you like. I don't know what mum's giving us to eat, but it goes with anything.'

'I'll be down presently,' she said sullenly and let out a sigh of relief when her father departed from the room.

She just wished that he and everyone else would leave her alone, though, ironically, it was the very fact of being left alone that had given her a gnawing grievance. It all went back to Jonathan's funeral.

She had convinced herself that she was madly in love with him and her initial reaction to his death had been one of grief mixed with intense bitterness. She had taken it for granted that they would marry and that her whole life would be suddenly transformed as by the wave of a wand. Accordingly she had gone to his funeral in the expectation of being treated as a close member of the family. She had insisted on going alone, to her

101

father's obvious pique, and was now at least thankful that she'd dissuaded her parents from accompanying her on what she had seen as a sort of sacred pilgrimage. Her humiliation had begun when, far from being treated as a near daughter-in-law, she found that none of his family appeared ever to have heard of her existence. Instead of being invited to sit with them at the service she was left to squeeze herself into a rear pew with a lot of red-eyed girls who had never even met Jonathan. Worse still, the wreath she had sent and which she had thought to see lying on his coffin was one of dozens piled against the outside wall of the church. When she tried to introduce herself to his agent, Paula Lang, she had received no more than a perfunctory word as that lady flitted about like a busy *maître d'hôtel*.

She had returned home bitterly disillusioned and determined to keep her feelings to herself. She had parried everyone's questions and allowed them to believe that it had all been just as she and they had previously supposed.

The day after her return from the funeral she had written to Jonathan's mother saying that she was the girl who had been with him on the evening of his death and how much in love they had been with each other. By way of reply she received a formal printed card thanking her for her sympathy in their tragic loss. On the back of the card his sister, Sheila, had written, 'We're grateful to all Jonathan's fans for their kind thoughts at this sad time.'

To be classed merely as one of his fans was the final humiliation.

There had followed a moment when she felt tempted to let a newspaper have her story – the story of her blazing love for Jonathan Cool and his passionate feelings towards her. That would certainly give his family a jolt. On the other hand if he hadn't got round to telling them of her existence in his life, it was hardly their fault. In the event, therefore, she kept her grievance to herself and continued quietly to nurse it. Meanwhile her feelings fluctuated from one extreme to another. At times she was sure she had meant as much to him as he had to her: at others, she was consumed with doubts and uncertainty and was ready to believe she had been no more than his plaything. The truth was there were facts to support both viewpoints.

And every day the trial ahead loomed a little closer.

Chapter 15

Two days after Sarah's visit, Rosa received a set of prosecution statements from the D.P.P. She was quickly satisfied that they were the same in content as those originally sent her by the police.

Typical piece of bureaucratic nonsense, she reflected, as she phoned the D.P.P.'s office to see if they could agree a timetable of events. She asked to speak to the Assistant Director who had called her in the first instance.

'My client is most anxious to have everything dealt with as quickly as possible,' she said when she was put through to him. 'The delay is clearly affecting her health. I shall be glad of your co-operation in getting things under way.'

'First things first, Miss Epton,' he said in a slightly condescending tone. 'We can hardly, for instance, try and expedite the trial until the committal proceedings have taken place.'

Rosa swallowed her annoyance at his tone and said, 'As you're aware, she stands remanded to appear before the magistrates on Tuesday the week after next. Is there any reason why we can't make that the date for committal?'

'That depends on what course you're proposing to take,' he said in the same superior tone. 'If you're willing to accept a Section One committal, I don't see any difficulty, but if there's any question of calling live evidence it mayn't be possible.'

'Why not?'

'Why not!' he echoed with a touch of asperity. 'Well, in the first place it probably won't suit the court and in the second because it mayn't be convenient to the prosecution. May I suggest that when you've had time to consider the statements, we have another word? If you decide you want any of the witnesses to give evidence in person, the court will presumably want to make special arrangements. The fact that you mayn't find yourself very popular with the clerk is your affair. Anyway give me another call when you've had time to think about it.'

There wasn't any visible smoke coming out of Rosa's ears when she replaced the receiver, but she felt there might have been. His tone and manner had thoroughly irked her. Moreover it caused her to review again the various options open to the defence.

Though her original thought had been to agree to a Section One (or paper) committal, she now began to wonder if there might not be virtue in seeking to destroy the prosecution's case at the earliest opportunity. That meant, in practice, destroying Cheryl Peterson's credibility. If that could be achieved, the magistrates should throw the case out, as there would be insufficient evidence to support a prima facie case. On the other hand, there was always a risk that the witness might emerge with her testimony strengthened by cross-examination before the actual trial.

Rosa glanced through the statements again. There was certainly no point in requiring any witness other than Cheryl to attend and give evidence before the magistrates. There was very little to dispute in what most of them said in their statements. She had met the clerk briefly on her previous appearance at the court and he had been both courteous and businesslike. She was sure he would be sympathetic to the option she was minded to take, even though it would consume more court time than otherwise.

But first she must get in touch with Sarah. She had little doubt what her response would be; indeed, it was her recollection of Sarah's slightly bitter reproach when Rosa had spoken against fighting the case in the magistrates' court that had caused her to think again. That and the Assistant Director's pedagogic manner.

Sarah answered the phone immediately and listened while Rosa explained her change of mind.

'You know how I feel,' she said. 'If you can get the case knocked out by the magistrates, it'd be wonderful. Any risk is worth taking to bring that about.' She paused. 'To think it could all be over in ten days' time!'

'Don't pitch your hopes too high! It won't be enough to dent Cheryl Peterson's evidence, it'll have to be totally discredited. And it'll need a strong bench not to take the easy option of sending the case forward to the crown court for a jury's decision.'

'I felt so depressed after my visit to your office the other day, but now you've raised my spirits,' Sarah said, as if she'd not listened to Rosa's caveat.

'I'm glad, but don't get too euphoric.'

'No, I do realise that it isn't all over yet.'

'Far from it, I'm afraid. Incidentally, have you been able to discuss things with Peter yet?'

'No. He has a way of forestalling me every time.'

'And he's not said anything to you about the case?'

'No. But I'm going to call him at the school and tell him what you're suggesting. I know he'll come to court with me that day. I suppose you might even want him to give evidence then?'

'It'll need thinking about,' Rosa said cautiously. 'Anything else to tell me before I ring off?'

Sarah gave a small laugh, more a release of tension than an expression of pleasure. 'We have workmen camped on the pavement outside, so that should keep Mr Peterson at bay. They've put up one of those canvas shelters and seem to spend most of their time brewing tea. I've yet to find out what they're supposed to be doing. They'll probably disappear leaving a large hole in the pavement as a reminder of their visit.' She paused. 'Apart from that, nothing new has happened.'

Rosa realised just how much her call had served to raise Sarah's morale. With this thought in mind she decided to phone the D.P.P.'s office immediately and tell him of the decision that had been reached.

'I've discussed the matter with my client,' she said when she'd been put through, 'and we want Cheryl Peterson to be called at the magistrates' court.'

'I see,' the Assistant Director said in a remote voice. 'Just her and nobody else?'

'Yes.'

'A Section Two committal in fact.'

'That's right.'

'I see,' he said again. 'Well, I suppose we'll have to try and find a date that's convenient to everyone. It clearly can't be the present remand date.'

'I can be ready by then.'

'Doubtless you can, Miss Epton, but it's a matter for the court – and the Director is also entitled to a say.'

'If the court can manage it that day, I take it the Director can.'

'I'm not committing myself.'

'But surely with your large staff you can find somebody to go to Worthing on Tuesday week?'

'As I said, I'm not committing myself. If it was going to be a Section One case, there'd obviously be no difficulty. But as you've elected for Section Two, I can't give any undertaking about dates. Incidentally, will you be briefing counsel?'

'No.'

'Doing the case yourself, eh?'

'Yes.'

'Hmm! Don't think I'm creating difficulties, Miss Epton, but it's not quite as simple as you appear to think. You clearly intend to cross-examine Miss Peterson and that, plus her examination-in-chief, is bound to occupy some time. It's not a question of everything being squeezed into half an hour.'

'I'm not suggesting it is.'

'What I don't understand is why you're in such a hurry. After all, the case is unlikely to reach trial at the crown court before March or April, or even early summer.'

'You're pre-supposing that the magistrates will commit it for trial,' Rosa observed.

'I see! So you're hoping to get it thrown out at the lower court, eh?'

'That's the object of the exercise.'

'It's a possibility that hadn't occurred to me. Miss Peterson's evidence seems so positive and clear.'

'So is my client's statement if you read it.'

'Defendants' statements are apt to be a trifle biased in their own favour.'

'Whereas all prosecution witnesses are the purveyors of pure truth, is that what you're saying?'

'I wouldn't go quite as far as that.'

'I believe there was once a judge, long before my time, I may say, who used always to refer to the *evidence* for the prosecution and the *story* for the defence when summing up to a jury.'

'I refrain from comment, Miss Epton. Anyway, I mustn't keep you talking. Leave the matter with me and I'll get in touch with you in due course.'

That was something Rosa had no intention of doing and she had barely put down the receiver before she picked it up again and made a call to the clerk's office at Worthing Magistrates' Court. She relayed her decision and expressed her hope that the committal proceedings could take place on Sarah's forthcoming appearance. For good measure she added that if it suited the court, she couldn't believe that the D.P.P. wouldn't also be able to find it convenient.

Now that the die was cast, she found herself looking forward with considerable zest to cross-examining Cheryl Peterson. It would be one of those make or break occasions and everything would depend on the skills she brought to the task.

Meanwhile the two workmen in the canvas shelter outside the Atkinses' house continued to brew tea and log all the comings and goings in the road.

Chapter 16

It didn't take long for Stan Peterson to get wind of what was happening. He was in the court's general office during the afternoon of Rosa's call and soon ferreted out the news.

His reaction was a mixture of surprise, agitation and belligerence. By the time he returned to Henner & Co. belligerence was his predominant mood. He put through an immediate call to someone he knew on the local paper and gave him the news.

'Wanted you to be the first to know,' he said sententiously. 'It's a quite extraordinary decision,' he went on with his usual air of authority. 'That woman solicitor must think she's something special. She's no hope of getting the case thrown out by the magistrates. My Cheryl's evidence will see to that. Anyway I'll leave you to pass the word around. Obviously the national press and the T.V. companies will want to be there now that there'll be something worth reporting. It'll serve that Epton woman right if she emerges with egg on her face. Must think she's some sort of Ophelia.'

'Don't you mean Portia?' his acquaintance said slyly. Like a good many others he didn't much care for Stan Peterson but regarded him as a useful contact.

'Ophelia, Portia, Lady Macbeth, take your choice,' Stan said, brushing aside what he saw as a quibble. 'The point is it's not going to do her client any good. You can tell anyone I said so.'

'I imagine Fleet Street and the television companies know already, or will do very shortly. Jonathan Cool's still news and any case concerning his death will bring them flocking.'

'Good! You've met my Cheryl, haven't you?'

'Yes.'

'She's a fine girl and she'll be an outstanding witness.'

'Maybe I could do an interview with her, once the case is over.'

'I'll bear it in mind.' In fact Stan had hopes that his daughter's story of shattered love would be taken up by one of the national papers. It certainly deserved, in his view, a far wider readership than any local paper could provide. And there was the money side to be thought of, too.

If Stan Peterson had anything to do with it, Sarah Atkins's trial was going to excel any circus; moreover, his Cheryl would be acknowledged as the star turn.

Since his trip to London, Mr Jameson had spent much time wondering what he should do next. Admittedly he had passed the baton to Rosa, but he was nagged by the feeling that he should make a further effort to try and unravel the deepening mystery surrounding Peter Atkins. One thing he did do was to turn again to his staff file and see what address Peter had written from when applying for the job. The letter was written in the hand now familiar to him and there was no doubt that it was Peter's. The address at the top was the Westview Private Hotel, Penney Road, London, W.4. In his letter Peter mentioned that he was a temporary resident but that a reply there would reach him. When Mr Jameson, on the day after the visit to London, phoned the hotel and asked to speak to the manager, that dignatory informed him that the hotel had undergone a change of ownership two years before and that the previous regime's records had vanished. After the frustration of the previous day, Mr Jameson wasn't particularly surprised at this further dead end to his enquiries.

On the day that Rosa talked to Sarah on the phone and subsequently notified the D.P.P. of the line the defence was preparing to take, Mr Jameson had decided there was only one thing for it. He must tackle Peter face to face and seek an explanation of his apparently false references. Having reached that bold conclusion, however, he decided he would approach the subject in a roundabout manner and so avoid any sort of head-on confrontation. He wasn't too sure how he was going to achieve this, but knew he must try.

Peter's last class that day finished at four-thirty and he would catch him as he came out, contriving to make it appear a casual encounter.

It was while he was in his study waiting for four-thirty to come round that he sipped a cup of tea and idly turned the pages of a newspaper one of the students had left in the hall. Suddenly his attention was caught by a sub-headline which read:

'Body of murdered man recovered from river.'

Mr Jameson picked the paper up to read what followed more easily.

The body of a man believed to be Stefan Jablonski aged about 54 was found in the River Thames near Woolwich ferry yesterday afternoon. Police say that preliminary examination shows he had been shot in the head and had been subjected to torture while still alive. He had been dead for at least twenty-four hours. Mr Jablonski is believed to have arrived in this country recently from Canada and police are anxious to trace his movements over the past week. Mr Jablonski used to live in North London until moving to Canada two years ago.

So far as it went the description exactly fitted the Mr Jablonski who had lived at 119 Sudmore Road before the Indian family took over the business. At all events, Mr Jameson had little doubt that they were one and the same person. On the other hand there was no reason to think that Mr Jablonski's sudden death was in any way connected with his earlier life in North London. It could only be a coincidence, if a somewhat chilling one. To Mr Jameson a vision of torture and then brutal murder implied a gangland killing, probably associated with some drugs deal. He knew that these days drugs were a multi-million pound business and that murder to such people was of no more consequence than blowing out a candle.

He was still thinking about Mr Jablonksi and his fate when he heard the door of Peter's classroom open and footsteps in the hall. He got up quickly from his desk and hurried out of the room.

111

'Hello, Peter,' he said a trifle breathlessly. 'I wonder if you can spare me a moment.'

'Certainly.'

'I'm not holding you up, I hope?' he went on in the same nervously breathless voice. 'Do phone Sarah from my study if you wish.'

A faintly puzzled frown passed across Peter Atkins's face.

'I'm not in any particular hurry,' he said in a reserved tone. 'I've no need to phone Sarah.'

'That's good! Come in and sit down. The thing is, I've got one of these awful forms to complete for the local adult education authority. Details of staff and that sort of thing and I can't for the life of me lay my hands on the particulars you supplied when you came here.' Mr Jameson sat down behind his desk and began shuffling papers. 'When was the date you joined the staff, Peter?'

'First of June nineteen seventy-nine.'

'And where had you been teaching previously?' Mr Jameson asked, busily scratching on a pad of paper.

'I hadn't. I'd been unemployed.'

'Ah, I'd forgotten that.' With a disarming smile, he went on, 'I obviously took up the references you gave, do you happen to remember who they were?'

Peter looked at him with mild surprise. 'The education authority wish to know that?' he enquired.

'I agree it's absurd, but our beloved bureaucrats have to send out these forms to justify their existence.' Mr Jameson accompanied the observation with an uneasy laugh.

'I see,' Peter said in a thoughtful voice. 'One of my references was a Miss Duxbury and the other was a bank manager. I think his name began with a P. Something like Parson or Purton.'

'Pearson perhaps.'

'Could be.'

'I suppose you've lost touch with him?'

'Yes.'

'And with Miss Duxbury?'

'She's dead.'

'Oh, I'm sorry. . . I . . .' Mr Jameson let the sentence tail off when Peter made no effort to come to his rescue. After an uncomfortable silence he said, 'Well, it seems the local authority will just have to be content with what we can tell them. They can hardly expect us to have memories like elephants just for their benefit.' When Peter still said nothing, he went on, 'What about a quick glass of sherry before you go? I know it's not yet five o'clock, but I like to think it's never too early for a decent sherry.'

'No, thank you, Jamie. I have to go into town before the shops close.'

'In that case I wonder if you can get something for me?'

'Of course,' Peter said civilly, but without enthusiasm.

'A refill for my ballpoint pen. Medium black is what I always have.' He passed the pen across to Peter as if to prove something or other.

'I'll buy you one and bring it in tomorrow.'

After Peter had left, Mr Jameson got up and drew the curtains across the windows. He knew he had mishandled the situation and he felt out of sorts with himself. His approach had lacked subtlety and deserved to fail. All it had achieved was to confirm that Peter had something to hide and that had been plain enough for some time past. As to what it might be Mr Jameson was no nearer discovering. His clumsy approach had aroused Peter's suspicions and in the circumstances he might have done better to have gone on and shown him the item about Stefan Jablonski's death and seen what reaction that produced.

A retired colleague of Geoffrey Traill's had recently moved to Findon, a few miles north of Worthing and it was there that Peter made his way after leaving Mr Jameson's. With the directions he had received, he found it without difficulty and parked outside.

A light was showing in the garage at the side of the bungalow and he could see items of furniture and a number of packing cases. A man was standing on a chair in the curtainless front room, apparently hammering a nail into the wall. By the time Peter reached the front door, the man had opened it.

'Peter Atkins?'

'Yes.'

113

'My name's also Peter, Peter Brookes. Come on in, Geoffrey should be here any minute. I'm afraid the place is still in chaos, but we only moved in two days ago. Incidentally, my wife's out.' He cocked an ear towards the door. 'That's probably Geoffrey now,' he said as he went back and opened it.

Traill stepped quickly inside and shook hands with both men.

'I was just explaining to Peter Atkins that the house is still in an awful mess,' the other Peter now went on. 'I think you'll be best off in the kitchen. At least the windows there have blinds. All the other rooms are still without curtains, thanks to the removal men putting them in the wrong van and despatching them, plus a lot of other things, to the other side of Colchester. They're due to arrive tomorrow, but anything could happen with the idiot packers we've engaged.'

'The kitchen will be fine,' Traill said. 'I'm sorry to impose on you like this, Peter, but it seemed heaven-sent with your living so close to our other Peter. Also there's a touch of urgency.'

'No need to apologise! The place is yours. My wife's out and after I've given you a drink, I'll leave you alone and get on with hammering nails into walls. What would you both like? I've got some beer and a bottle of vermouth, otherwise it's tea or coffee. Most of the booze has also gone off to Colchester.'

'Coffee for me, please,' Peter Atkins said. 'Black and no sugar.'

'I'd like the same, but with a dash of milk,' Traill said.

While Peter Brookes was making the coffee, he and Geoffrey Traill discussed the merits of gas or electric central heating. Peter Atkins listened in grave silence.

'Right, I'll leave you to it,' Brookes now said, picking up a mug of coffee and departing.

'Don't think he's quite closed the door,' Traill remarked, going over and giving it a firm push until there was a click. He returned and sat down at the table where Peter was already seated, and gave him a slightly cautious smile. He had a youthful, almost cherubic face with very fair, ultra-fine hair that lay quite flat on his head. He looked much younger than his thirty-eight years. 'So how are things with Sarah?' he asked.

'Difficult. . . . Not at all easy. . . she doesn't understand what's

114

going on.'

'You know she tried to see me?'

Peter threw him a sharp look. 'What do you mean?'

'She phoned me a few days ago and said she wanted to talk to me about you.'

Peter let out a small groan. 'But you didn't meet her?'

Traill shook his head as if the question were superfluous. 'I agreed at first, but later rang her at Rosa Epton's office and said I'd been called away to an urgent meeting. She didn't tell you any of this?'

'No. I knew she went up to London to see Miss Epton, but she said nothing about phoning you.'

'As a matter of fact she said she didn't want you to know that she'd got in touch with me,' Traill remarked with a thin smile.

'How did she get hold of your telephone number?'

'Presumably you must have written it down somewhere and she found it.' Traill's tone carried a note of reproof.

'But I haven't. I keep it in my head. It was on your letter – the one you wrote at my request asking me to come and see you – but I tore that up and threw it away.'

'She must have pieced it together. Anyway, no great harm has been done, but it shows you can never afford to lower your guard.'

Peter shook his head miserably.

'Life's very difficult at the moment.'

'It's been worse,' Traill said with a hard glittering smile which vanished as quickly as it came. 'The question is what to do.'

'I thought everything had been settled.'

'Unfortunately not. The situation is what one might call fluid.'

'Mr Jameson also suspects something,' Peter said bleakly. 'He's been asking questions about my application to join his staff. He wanted to know if I could remember the names I gave as references. Pretended he'd lost my file and needed the information to fill in a form.'

Traill stared across the kitchen with a thoughtful frown. 'We must be prepared to lay a false trail for Mr Jameson if he gets too inquisitive. We must also think what to do about Sarah. Things

115

are becoming unstitched in awkward places. Incidentally, have you seen a newspaper today?' Peter shook his head. 'Then you won't have read that Stefan Jablonski has been found murdered. You remember him?'

'Yes.'

'His body was fished out of the river at Woolwich. He'd been tortured before being shot in the back of the head.'

'I thought he'd gone to Canada.'

'He did. The questions, therefore, to be answered are, what brought him back, who knew he was returning and what did he tell anyone under torture?'

'Did he have anything worth telling?'

'Somebody obviously thought so. His death, of course, mayn't have any connection with what concerns you and me. Anyway, let's hope not! On the other hand, once you shake the apple tree you may get something apart from the expected apples falling at your feet.' He gave Peter a knowing wink. 'It'll clearly be unwise for me to call you at home for a while and you'd better tell Sarah I've gone abroad. I'll have the number she got me on disconnected.' He gave Peter a sudden grin. 'In a few years time I'll be ready myself for a nice gentle job at Mr Jameson's, meanwhile I'll find out just what the old boy's been up to.' His expression changed and he shook his head with a resigned air. 'There wasn't a cloud on the horizon before Sarah had that accident. Why, oh why, did it have to be Jonathan Cool?'

Chapter 17

Rosa had been asking herself the same question from a different angle without coming up with any sort of an answer; namely, what was there about Jonathan Cool's death to cause Peter Atkins to react as he had?

She had delved into Cool's family life and background (there was no shortage of source material), but had failed to uncover anything that resembled even the most tenuous link between him and Peter. She had made discreet enquiries about his parents, Mr and Mrs Coolie, only to learn that they were pillars of middle-class respectability. Mr Coolie worked in an accountant's office, his wife had a part-time job in a dress shop. Sheila, their daughter and only other child, worked on a newspaper in Leicester and came home one weekend a month. It seemed their family life could be summed up by one word, blameless. Not that Rosa necessarily assumed it was so, but she failed to see how she could take her enquiries any further in that direction. So once more she asked herself, why had Jonathan Cool's death had this strange effect on Peter Atkins?

When she arrived in the office the next morning she was pleased to find Robin already there. They had been boxing and coxing for the best part of a week and she'd not had an opportunity of discussing recent developments with him.

He gave her a welcoming smile as she entered his room and sat down.

'You've come to tell me that all is now clear and that your case fits together like a precision watch,' he observed with one eyebrow cocked.

'If you weren't my senior partner, I'd say something extremely rude. First of all, have you learnt on the office grapevine that I'm opting for a Section Two committal and requiring the girl, Cheryl Peterson, to give her evidence live at the magistrates' court?'

'Stephanie told me the other evening when I called her from court and asked for a round-up of office news.'

'I just hope I've made the right decision and given Sarah Atkins sound advice,' Rosa said in a doubtful voice. 'I wish I could have discussed it with you first, Robin, but you were never around when I needed you.'

He was about to make a facetious comment, but realised Rosa was not in the mood.

'Why do you have doubts about your decision?'

'Because I was stung into making it by the Assistant Director to whom I spoke. I wanted to show him that solicitors didn't always do what the D.P.P. expected. I wanted to dent his complacence.'

'And did you?'

'He didn't seem very pleased when I called him back and told him what I'd decided. He addressed me from a great height and in effect said be it on my own head.'

'I assume Sarah Atkins was happy to accept your advice?'

'She was delighted. That was another factor I had in mind. I knew she was depressed by the prospect of the long wait before trial and would jump at the suggestion of fighting the case at the preliminary hearing. She'd expressed her disappointment when I'd originally advised that an uncontested committal was the right course. She's always wanted to do battle at the earliest moment.' She gave her partner a tentative look. 'Do you think I've been rash, Robin? Made the wrong decision for wrong reasons?'

'Only time will show that,' he remarked with a thoughtful air. 'Obviously there are risks. Everything depends on Cheryl Peterson's performance in the witness box.'

'I'm sure I can shake her,' Rosa broke in. 'I know she's lying.'

'If she's not, then it has to be Sarah Atkins.'

118

Rosa shook her head vigorously. 'I'm convinced she's telling the truth. And you know I'm not easily taken in by a client's story.'

Robin Snaith accepted this as a general truth, though he could think of occasions when his junior partner's head had not always been in charge of the decision-making process. There'd been times when she had become emotionally involved with clients, usually feckless and amoral young men heavily endowed with impudent charm. There was no question, however, of Sarah Atkins falling into that category.

'If you succeed in discrediting Cheryl Peterson's evidence so that the magistrates take the view no reasonable jury could accept it, they're bound to throw the case out and your decision will have been justified one hundred per cent. But it's a large "if".'

'And if I fail to do that?'

'If you fail the case will go for trial at the crown court.'

'You know I didn't mean that, Robin. If I fail, what'll be the possible repurcussions?'

'I'm sure you've worked them out for yourself already.'

'I may have overlooked something.'

'The most serious, as I see it,' he went on after a slight pause, 'is that Cheryl Peterson will emerge with her evidence enhanced. She'll come through as such a patently truthful witness that, unless she drops dead between committal and trial, you've lost the case before you ever get to the crown court.'

'Even if I fail to make any impression on her as a witness, I'll still not believe she's telling the truth.'

'You're being too subjective.'

'I know,' she said unhappily. 'If I don't succeed in getting the case thrown out at the lower court, I'll have to brief a counsel who knows how to cross-examine a scheming, lying witness.'

'His job will be easier than yours, anyway. It's far harder to get magistrates to accept a submission of no case to answer than it is to persuade a jury to acquit. And you're not going to get any help from a half-hearted prosecution. If you do manage to chip pieces off Miss Peterson, the prosecution will certainly try and put her

119

together again in re-examination.'

'Unless I can totally discredit her evidence and show her up as a perjurer.'

'You'll have to do all of that.'

Rosa was pensive for a while. 'Do you really think I'm on to a humiliating loser?'

'If I believed the course you're proposing to take spelt total disaster, I'd say so. I do think the odds are against you, but that's different from saying you're heading for a certain tumble. Forensic tactics aren't dissimilar to those on the battlefield. There are risks whatever you do. Should you or should you not call this or that witness? How much should you stress a particular point? Can you safely take your cross-examination any farther? They're decisions we're making all the time, and hoping for the best. You've decided to have a fight in the magistrates' court, so good luck to you. At least there'll be no recriminations from your client if you fail. Incidentally, do you propose to call her to give evidence at that stage?'

Rosa shook her head. 'No. The court will have her written statement as part of the prosecution case and if I can't destroy Cheryl Peterson's evidence, that'll be that. Nothing Sarah might then say in the box is going to influence them on the issue of a case to answer.'

'So you'll have no occasion to call her husband until the case reaches trial – if it does. Incidentally, has he been exhibiting any further signs of aberrant behaviour?'

Robin listened attentively while Rosa related Mr Jameson's discoveries.

'What's the explanation?' he asked in a mystified tone when she had finished.

'I wish I knew. I begin to wonder if he's caught up in some major criminal activity which could be jeopardised by his wife's case, or, and this is just as far-fetched, he's a member of one of the intelligence services and his wife's trial will in some way make him vulnerable to exposure.'

Robin shook his head doubtfully. 'Neither makes great sense,' he remarked.

'What's your theory then?'

For a while he was silently thoughtful. 'This is even more far-fetched,' he said at length, 'but it seems to fit his conduct rather better. Supposing he's a sleeper. You know, a foreign agent planted here and left to his own quiet devices until somebody in Moscow or wherever presses a button and activates him.'

Rosa frowned as she pondered this novel suggestion. 'You're right, Robin, it fits his conduct better than either of my ideas. It explains his fake references when he joined Mr Jameson's and his general air of mystery, not least his reluctance to become involved in a court case in this country. It means, of course, that Peter Atkins isn't his real name.' She gave her partner an admiring look. 'That's a terribly ingenious idea, Robin.'

'It could be miles off course. And even if it isn't, where does it take you? You can't tax him with it, nor is it your business to put the idea into his wife's head. You're only concerned with defending her on a motoring charge, not on uncovering her husband's past life.'

'I'm quite certain she doesn't know. She's genuinely upset and worried by his behaviour. That's not an act on her part.'

'So whether I'm right or wrong has no real bearing on your case.'

'If he is a sleeper, shouldn't the security service be informed?'

Robin gave her a look of alarm. 'There'll be time enough to consider that when the case is over. In any event all you could do would be to voice speculation. It doesn't even amount to suspicion as yet.' He reached for the dictionary that lay with various law books on a table beside his desk. ' "Sleeper",' he read out. ' "A communist or other agent who spends a long time, often years, establishing himself as an inoffensive citizen preparing for the moment when he will be required to pass on a particular vital piece of information." End of quote.' He glanced up and gave Rosa a quizzical look. 'Could just as well fit you or me!'

'Not as well as it fits Peter Atkins,' she said eagerly.

'As you're unlikely ever to uncover the truth, and as it's not relevant to your case, I wouldn't let it occupy too much of your time.' But he could tell from her expression that she wouldn't let the matter drop. 'Be careful, Rosa,' he urged. 'Remember your priorities and don't go probing just to satisfy your personal curiosity. If he *is* a sleeper, it could be dangerous.'

Chapter 18

Sarah usually gave Nicole her lunch around half-past twelve and ate her own at the same time. Nicole's was the more elaborate meal of the two, Sarah contenting herself with leftovers from the fridge. She and Peter had their main meal in the evening.

By one o'clock Nicole was up in her bedroom having a rest and Sarah would have a luxurious hour's reading. The telephone seldom rang between one and two and nobody ever came to the door.

On the day in question she had just kicked off her shoes and put her feet up on the settee, and was finding her place in the novel she had got out of the library the previous day, when the front door bell rang.

She stood up with a fretful sigh and walked quietly across to the window to catch a glimpse of her visitor. She certainly wasn't expecting anyone. To her annoyance whoever it was stood too close to the front door to be observed. She was wondering whether to lie low and pretend to be out when the bell rang again and the caller stepped back and came into view. Sarah stepped out of sight before he could spot her. At least she now knew her visitor was male. He looked neatly dressed and generally presentable. If it hadn't been for recent events she might still have let him go on ringing the bell until he got tired and departed. Her curiosity was aroused, however, and in the unlikely hope that he might somehow cast light on her doubts she put on her shoes and went to open the door. It had also flashed through her mind that her visitor might be Geoffrey Traill, come to make amends for cancelling their meeting. A brief glimpse of the man standing at the door was not unlike the picture of

Geoffrey she carried in her mind's eye.

She had just reached the door when the bell rang a third time, insistent and demanding as though her visitor knew she was at home and had no intention of leaving.

'Mrs Atkins?' he said with a note of polite enquiry when she opened the door. He looked near enough her own age and was wearing a narrow-brimmed brown hat, a paisley silk scarf and a camel hair coat. Sarah noticed for the first time that he was carrying a slim document case in his right hand.

'Yes,' she replied warily.

'I hope I've not called at a very inconvenient time,' he went on pleasantly, 'but I know it's a generally good hour to catch ladies of the house at home. My name's Andrew Strong and I represent the Norrington Comprehensive Insurance Company.' He flashed her a quick disarming smile. 'I assure you, Mrs Atkins, I'm not trying to sell you anything on the doorstep; we don't believe in that sort of crude approach at Norrington. What I'd like to do is leave you some of our literature which you can read at your leisure and discuss with your husband and then I'll call again in about a week's time. By then I'm sure you'll have found one of our schemes to meet your particular needs.' He paused. 'Would it be possible for me to come in for just a few minutes?'

Sarah looked at him with an air of uncertainty. 'I really don't think. . .'

'Oh dear,' he exclaimed suddenly diving a hand into his coat pocket, 'I'm always forgetting to prove my bona fides. Here's my company identity card!'

He held it out for Sarah to take. She glanced at it in some embarrassment. It bore his photograph and was signed by the managing director of the Norrington Comprehensive Insurance Company who said he had great pleasure in introducing Mr Andrew Strong to the world at large. The address was a box number at Kingston-upon-Thames.

'I'm afraid I'm rather busy at the moment,' she said in a wavering tone. 'I have to take my daughter out in a few minutes.'

'Just give me five minutes, Mrs Atkins,' he said in an almost pleading voice, at the same time preparing to step inside. 'I

124

promise not to overstay.' As Sarah led the way into the living-room, he continued to talk. 'My company's in a position to offer particularly advantageous terms to new clients. It's all part of a promotional campaign we're conducting on the south coast. We're not an enormous company but we're certainly go-ahead and are able to give far greater personal service than the giants in the business.' He had taken off his coat and he now glanced quickly about him.

'What a pleasant residential area this is! The sea an easy car-ride away and the Downs at your back door,' he continued with effortless momentum. 'You mentioned a daughter, Mrs Atkins, might I ask what age she would be?'

'Just over two.'

'May I also enquire your husband's occupation?' he asked making jottings in a black notebook.

'He's a teacher.'

'How I admire teachers! I could never have been one. Haven't the patience.' He glanced around the room. 'Would that be his photograph on the television set?'

'No. That was my brother. He was killed in a plane crash several years ago.'

'Oh, I'm sorry. I somehow took it for granted it was a photograph of your husband. That must be one of your daughter on the mantelpiece, yes?'

'Yes, that's Nicole.'

He continued to gaze round the room. 'Some people like to be surrounded by family photographs and others shove them into drawers. But I mustn't keep you.' He opened his document case and took out a folder. 'The best thing will be for me to leave you this. It contains details of all our schemes and then when I call next time we can discuss the one that interests you most.' He glanced at his watch. 'I promised I wouldn't stay more than five minutes, Mrs Atkins, and I won't.' He closed his document case with a brisk snap and jumped to his feet. 'Thank you for giving me your time; I'm sure you won't regret it. Indeed it's my bet that when your husband reads what's in that folder, he'll commend you for having listened to me.'

125

'Are you calling at all the houses in this road?' Sarah enquired as she accompanied him to the front door.

'No, we select which homes to visit very carefully. We have an efficient market research department and we do our homework before we ever make a call. Otherwise one can waste so much valuable time.' He threw her a smile as between two people with a common interest. 'The last thing one wants to do is squander one's resources. Everything is designed to be maximum cost-effective. Does your husband have far to go to work?' he asked casually as they reached the door.

'He teaches at a language school in Swift Road.'

'Ah! So he doesn't come home worn out by a classroom of rowdy kids.' He held out his hand. 'Thank you again, Mrs Atkins. It's been a pleasure meeting you and I'll be back in a week or ten days. Incidentally, is it all right to come at this same hour?'

'I'm usually at home.'

'Fair enough. Anyway, I'll phone you in advance.'

'That would be better.'

With a final wave of his hand he turned and walked with a purposeful step down the path to the front gate. Sarah closed the door and returned to the living-room, exhausted by his almost non-stop flow of words. She couldn't help reflecting what a poor salesman, by comparison, Peter would make.

She wondered whether Peter might phone her before he went back into class that afternoon. Until recently he had always done so just before two o'clock, but Sarah had failed to comment the first time he lapsed and he had certainly not offered any explanation. She found herself torn two ways, both wanting to precipitate a crisis in their relationship and yet avoid one.

As she gazed at the folder her visitor had left on the table, she had a sudden urge to call Peter and tell him what had happened, but in his present mood he would probably think she had an ulterior motive. In fact all she had was a deep, deep yearning for the comfortable relationship they had previously enjoyed. She had often read of people being in a state of suspended animation and had herself glibly used the expression, but she now realised

126

how exactly it described her present situation.

She heard Nicole call out and went upstairs. Christmas was only a month away and she was dreading it. So much could happen between now and then. Her life had been subjected to a major earthquake and now there were almost daily tremors.

She and Nicole were sitting on the floor drawing cats for each other when Peter came in just after five o'clock. A slow smile spread across his face as he looked through the living-room door and saw them. He held out his arms when Nicole jumped up and ran across to him. He bent down to give her a hug. Then he came over to where Sarah was kneeling on the floor and kissed her upturned face.

'A good day?' she enquired with a slight lump in her throat.

He grimaced. 'I'm getting tired of teaching English to Spanish and Italian waiters,' he remarked sourly.

'Has something in particular happened?' Sarah asked with a worried frown.

'No. I just think it's time I had a change.'

Her heart skipped a beat. What was coming now?

'Such as?'

'I've no idea. But I feel unsettled.'

'You've not had any trouble with Jamie?'

'What makes you ask that?' His tone was suddenly wary.

'Nothing, except that having been his secretary I know he can be difficult at times.'

'You wouldn't mind a move, would you?' he asked in a matter-of-fact voice as though it was something they had already discussed.

'What a time to ask!' she remarked with a touch of asperity. 'Anyway, where to? Why are you suddenly talking like this, Peter?'

'Once the case is over, we'll move right away.'

Sarah shook her head in bewilderment. 'I don't know what to say. I'm not sure how serious you are.'

She felt she was being battered by gales coming from different directions. It was one thing to have Peter suddenly talking about their future, another to contemplate a total upheaval in their

127

lives.

'It'll probably be a good thing to move right away,' he said, giving the impression that his mind was already made up. His eye lit upon the folder lying on the table. 'What's that?'

'A representative of the Norrington Comprehensive Insurance Company called here at lunchtime and left some literature for us to read. He's coming back in a week's time to find out if we're interested in any of their schemes. I didn't hold out any hope that we would be.'

Peter had listened with an impassive expression, but his next question took Sarah by surprise.

'What did he look like?'

'Clean, well-dressed, polite. Perfectly respectable, or I wouldn't have let him in.'

'How old?'

'Early thirties.'

'What was he wearing?'

'He had on a camel hair coat and a grey suit and suede shoes. And he was wearing a slightly fuzzy brown hat. But why are you so interested in his appearance?'

'Did he ask you anything about me?' he went on, ignoring her question.

'Only in a casual sort of way,' she said defensively. 'I told him you taught at a language school.'

'Did you say where?'

'I believe I said in Swift Road. Was that very wrong of me?' She had the sensation of standing on the edge of a chasm. 'Look, Peter,' she burst out, 'we've got to talk. We can't go on like this.'

He frowned and glanced down at Nicole who was unconcernedly drawing another cat.

'I know just how you're feeling, my darling,' he said, turning towards her and putting out a hand to stroke her face with his fingertips. 'All this waiting is playing hell with your nerves. It's not surprising you get upset and can't see things straight.'

Sarah stepped back from him. 'It's no good, Peter, we've got to have things out.'

'Ssh, you'll frighten Nicole,' he said in a lowered voice.

128

'As soon as Nicole's in bed, we're going to have a talk,' she remarked determinedly.

'I'll get you a drink and then I'll take Nicole up to bed.'

'But we're still going to have a talk. It can't be put off any longer.'

Nicole, however, seemed in no hurry to go to bed, nor Peter to take her upstairs. When eventually they did leave the room, Sarah sat fidgeting with her glass waiting for her husband to return. It seemed an age before she heard his footsteps on the stairs. She steeled herself to face the door. He gave her a quick sidelong glance as he entered.

'We'll have a look at what that insurance man left,' he said as he walked across and picked up the folder.

'That can wait, Peter! Come and sit down and listen to me!' Her voice sounded unnatural to her own ears and her skin felt as if it had been stretched tight across her forehead. 'Something's happened to you, Peter. Please, please tell me what it is, as it's useless to go on pretending that everything's all right.'

'Of course everything's not all right with you under all this strain.'

'It's not me, it's you. Something's happened to *you*. Something you're keeping hidden from me.'

'You're seeing everything out of perspective,' he said with a sigh. 'Harmless shadows have become frightening ghosts. Tomorrow I'll take you to see Dr Williams; I'm sure he'll give you some tranquillisers.'

'Why won't you tell me the truth, Peter?' she cried out in anguish. 'I know you're concealing something from me.'

'What am I supposed to be concealing?' he asked in an unyielding tone.

'You've been behaving strangely ever since the accident.'

He frowned. 'If so, it's because I'm worried on your account. I know you're suffering, which means that I'm suffering, too.' He paused. 'You mustn't become paranoid, my darling.'

'Nor must you!'

'Me?'

'Yes, look how suspicious you became when I told you about

129

the insurance man's visit.'

'I don't like strangers coming to the door when you're alone in the house.'

'Is that all?' she enquired. 'Then why did you want to know what he looked like and whether he asked any questions about you?'

'I was trying to decide whether we should inform the police. He could easily have been a burglar making a reconnaissance.'

'I hardly think a burglar would have shown any interest in family photographs,' she remarked.

'What photographs?'

'He wanted to know if that one of Stephen was you. I told him it was my brother.'

For a few seconds, Peter stared across the room with an expression of intense concentration. Then he turned and hurried out.

'Where are you going?' Sarah called out anxiously.

'I'll be back soon,' he said, almost at the same moment as she heard the front door open and close. She dashed out and flung it open in time to see him hurrying away along the pavement.

Alarmed and bewildered, she returned to the living-room. He could have gone out for one purpose only, to make a telephone call he didn't wish her to overhear.

As she awaited his return, her mood once more became grimly determined. At least he could no longer pretend that it was all in her imagination. His behaviour that evening was conclusive proof that something was seriously amiss in his life.

Half an hour went by and then the phone rang. As she heard Peter's voice she was torn by a mixture of relief and anxiety.

'It's me, my darling,' he said in a carefully controlled tone. 'I may be out a bit longer than I thought, but don't worry!'

'Peter, where are you? What's happened?'

'I'm all right, so don't worry. I can't talk more now. . .'

'Please tell me what's happened?' she cried out desperately.

'I'll see you soon,' he said and rang off.

She knew she must keep a tight grasp on her emotions and not surrender to hysteria. Cool thought was essential. As she glanced round she noticed that the insurance company's folder had vanished. Peter must have taken it with him. But why?

She was gratified, and surprised, how calm she managed to remain. She went into the kitchen and scrambled some eggs for her supper. She removed the casserole which was to have been their evening meal from the oven. She even found herself wondering whether she would ever see Peter again. No thought seemed too fanciful.

After she had eaten, she contemplated phoning Mr Jameson, but decided to wait until the morning. If Peter had returned by then, it wouldn't be necessary anyway.

At half-past ten she decided to go up to bed and take a sleeping pill, though she doubted whether it would have the desired effect. She had just switched off the downstairs lights when the phone rang.

'Sarah?' said a familiar, cheerful voice. 'It's Geoffrey Traill. I just wanted to reassure you that Peter's fine, apart from being worried about you. He'll be in touch with you very shortly. . .'

'Where is he?' Sarah asked with renewed agitation.

'He's with me.'

'But where?'

'He sends you all his love. I must ring off now.'

She made her way upstairs to bed feeling drained of any emotion. She was only aware of having a throbbing headache.

The first thing she noticed when she pulled back the curtains the next morning was that the workmen had returned – and were ensconced in their canvas shelter on the pavement outside. They were already busy brewing tea, their kettle spouting steam. As she watched a hand came out through a flap in the canvas and reached for the kettle.

131

Chapter 19

As soon as Sarah had given Nicole her breakfast and settled her on the living-room floor with paper and pencil (how she blessed her daughter's absorption in endlessly drawing animals. She might never be a Stubbs or a Landseer but it wouldn't be for lack of concentrated effort) she telephone Mr Jameson.

'Peter won't be coming in today, Jamie,' she said, leaving him to ask the inexorable question.

'Sick, is he?'

'No. He's had to go away.' She paused before going on with a rush. 'Don't ask me where or why, because I don't know.' After which she proceeded to tell him what had happened the previous evening.

'Oh dear, oh dear, my poor Sarah! I am sorry. What a worry! Of course I'm not as surprised as I might have been for I've realised there's been something odd, very odd indeed, about Peter's behaviour.' He then related his efforts to check her husband's references and ended up by mentioning the newspaper report of Stefan Jablonski's death. 'I didn't tell you before because it seemed to me you had worries enough, but I did take the liberty of informing Rosa Epton.'

'Did you say anything to Peter about what you'd found out?'

'I tried to tackle him, but I'm afraid I did it very ineptly and I think I aroused his suspicions.' He paused. 'Your case comes up the day after tomorrow, doesn't it?'

'Yes.'

'He's sure to be back by then.'

'We'll see,' Sarah said bleakly.

'I can't believe Peter would ever let you down.'

132

'He refused to go to court with me the last time,' Sarah remarked. 'After all, Jamie, I'm now certain that the reason he doesn't want to give evidence or be seen anywhere near a court is because he's frightened of being recognised.'

'By whom?'

'He's obviously mixed up in something or other and is terrified of any publicity.'

'I refuse to believe it's anything disgraceful,' Mr Jameson said stoutly. 'Peter's a gentleman.' After a pause he went on, 'Perhaps he once worked for one of our intelligence agencies. That would explain the funny business about his references and why he's gone to ground just after this man Jablonski has been found murdered. His friend, Geoffrey Traill, obviously belongs to the same outfit as Peter. It must be something along those lines, Sarah. He's obviously sworn to secrecy – those chaps always are – and can't tell you what's going on, however much he'd like to. Why don't you have a word with Rosa Epton?'

'I'm going to. She may be able to find out something. Anyway, Jamie, thank you for your words of comfort. I just wish I could make more sense out of it.'

'Phone me whenever you want and remember that everything will come all right in the end.'

'I never thought I'd hear you say anything so Pollyanna-ish.'

'Well, it's true of my own life,' he proclaimed firmly. 'And I was eighty last birthday.'

'I know. It was the day I had my accident.'

After satisfying herself that Nicole was still happily drawing, Sarah returned to the telephone and put through a call to Rosa. She had told her daughter that her father had had to go away suddenly in the night but would be back soon and Nicole had accepted this.

'Hello, Rosa,' she said on being connected. 'I've just been talking to Mr Jameson and he advised me to have a word with you. I was going to do so in any event.' Like many people she found it easier to break ominous news affecting herself in a circumlocutory fashion. 'I hope I'm not phoning at an

133

inconvenient time?'

'No, go ahead! What's happened?'

'My husband's gone away,' she said with some embarrassment. 'Gone away' sounded less dramatic than plain 'gone' or
'disappeared'. With the ice broken she gave Rosa a recital of the
previous day's events. 'Incidentally,' she said in conclusion,
'Jamie's told me that he got in touch with you after his abortive
visit to London.'

'Yes, he did.'

'I'm in a state of total bewilderment, Rosa. I don't know what
to make of Peter's behaviour.'

'I think it's probably time I told you that he visited me in the
office about two weeks ago. Did he ever mention that?'

'Never. What did he want?' Sarah asked dully.

'He said he wasn't really in a position to give any evidence as
he was asleep when the accident happened.'

'But that's not true,' Sarah burst out. 'How could he say that?'

'Well, he did; not that I believed him. In any event I told him
that, even so, it would be necessary to call him as a witness to
prove the fact in order to prevent the jury drawing any damaging
conclusions. After all they'd know he'd been in the car with you.'
She paused. 'Why do you think he's so desperately anxious not to
get drawn into the case?'

'Jamie thinks he's working for MI5 or one of that lot and is
worried about the publicity his appearance in court might
attract. Do you think that's a possibility?'

'Yes, I suppose it could be,' Rosa said. She was not going to
suggest to Sarah that her husband could be a foreign spy who had
been planted here and was awaiting a call to action.

'If not, what other explanation is there?'

'I can't think of anything,' Rosa replied vaguely. Fortunately,
she reflected, Peter's disappearance need have no effect on her
conduct of the case in the magistrates' court.

'I was wondering if the D.P.P. might tell you anything,' Sarah
went on. 'Couldn't you try and get him to drop you a hint?'

'I doubt whether he'd take me into his confidence, even if he
knows anything.'

'It occurred to me that was why he'd taken the case over. Because Peter worked secretly for MI5.'

'I wonder,' Rosa said in a thoughtful voice. 'I'll try and think whether there's any approach I can properly make. I'll call you tomorrow, Sarah, and if you still have no news of Peter I'll drive down to Worthing in the evening and perhaps we could have a meal together and put the finishing touches to next day's court appearance.'

'We have a spare room, so why not stop the night here?' Sarah said eagerly.

'That would be fine. I have to dash off to court now, but we'll talk again shortly.'

On her way out of the office Rosa poked her head round Robin's door and told him the latest news. He listened to her in silence before offering any comment.

'If I were you,' he said, 'I'd forget that Peter Atkins ever existed.'

'But I'd still like to know what he's up to.'

'I know you would, but satisfying your personal curiosity is not part of your professional duty in defending his wife.'

Rosa knew that Robin was right even though he stated the issue in its most simplistic form. Nevertheless she decided that when she returned from court she would phone the D.P.P.'s department and see what she could find out. It was mid-afternoon before the opportunity arose.

'It's Rosa Epton of Snaith and Epton,' she said on being put through to the Assistant Director with whose cool, superior tones she was now familiar. 'I was ringing to ask who will be representing you at court on Friday?'

'We've instructed counsel. Mr Robert Gidman will be appearing on behalf of the Director.'

Rosa had never come across Gidman in court, but knew him to be a senior member of his circuit and someone who often appeared for the prosecution in the role of trouble-shooter.

'Oh! So it won't be one of your own staff doing the case?' she remarked in a tone of surprise.

'No.'

'It sounds as if you're taking a sledgehammer to crack a nut,' she said with a small self-deprecating laugh.

'Nuts come in all shapes and sizes, don't they, Miss Epton? Not to mention their varying thickness of shell.'

'Would I be right in thinking that you've upgraded your representation because of my decision to fight the case in the lower court?'

'Who said anything about upgrading it?' he asked in the tone that Rosa found so irritating. 'We not infrequently instruct counsel in the magistrates' court. There can be any number of reasons for doing so. You'd be quite wrong to infer it's because we regard the case as beyond the forensic skills of our own staff.'

'I never meant to suggest that,' Rosa said hastily. 'I realise the case is bound to attract a lot of publicity, as well as having some delicate features. . .'

But the Assistant Director declined to be drawn and Rosa decided she must either adopt a more blunt approach or let the matter drop.

'You mayn't feel disposed to answer this,' she went on in her most honeyed tone, 'but I wonder if you have anything in your files concerning my client's husband, Peter Atkins? I'd be grateful for anything you can pass on to me, if necessary in confidence and off the record. I don't want to find myself in any embarrassment over calling him as a witness.'

'I'm afraid I can't tell you anything either on or off the record, Miss Epton,' he said briskly.

'May I take it then that you have nothing on him?'

'I have nothing further to add.'

'Well, I mustn't keep you any longer. Will I see you at court?'

'No, but one of our professional staff will be there instructing counsel.'

'May I ask who?'

'Jennie Passmore.'

'I don't think I've met her.'

'I'm sure you'll be well matched, Miss Epton.'

When Rosa later reported this conversation to Robin, he repeated what he had previously said. 'Forget Peter Atkins!

Whatever the Director knows about him he's not going to tell you. You've had your fishing expedition and caught an old boot.'

'I still think you're right about his being a sleeper,' Rosa said thoughtfully. 'I wonder if the authorities are on to him. The Assistant Director was distinctly cagey and non-committal. I felt he knew something, but wasn't going to say.'

'There's such a thing as tactics,' Robin observed. 'Because he chose to fence with you doesn't necessarily mean he has anything to hide. My advice to you remains the same: forget Peter Atkins!'

Rosa gave her senior partner an abstracted nod and departed. Robin had, in fact, reached his own fresh conclusion concerning Sarah's husband. He thought it increasingly likely that he was somebody who had served a sentence for murder (probably wife-murder) and on release from prison had assumed a new name in his effort to live down his past and start a completely fresh life. This seemed to him rather less fanciful than the sleeper theory and yet would explain much, including Peter Atkins's somewhat obscure background.

He had not thought it advisable to put the idea into Rosa's head. Her imagination was lively enough without any further stimulation.

Chapter 20

Rosa was about to leave the office to drive down to Worthing the next evening when Stephanie announced that Mr Atkins was on the line and would like to speak to her.

'Do you mean Peter Atkins?' Rosa asked.

'All he said was Mr Atkins,' Stephanie replied in her most detached voice. 'I assume it's the one who came to see you.'

'That's Peter Atkins.'

'Very likely, but I've never met him so wouldn't know. I was out when he came here.'

'You'd better put him through,' Rosa said with a mixture of feelings. What on earth could Peter Atkins be phoning to tell her?

'Rosa Epton speaking,' she said a moment later.

'It's Peter Atkins, Miss Epton.' He spoke in the quick, hushed tone of someone who was afraid of being overheard. 'I wanted to wish you all the best in court tomorrow. It'll be an enormous relief if you can get Sarah off. . .'

'Have you spoken to her today?' Rosa broke in.

'Not yet. I. . .'

'Where are you now?' she broke in again.

'I'm with a friend.'

'Would that be Geoffrey Traill?'

'Please, Miss Epton, I can't answer questions.'

'You realise that if your wife's convicted, it'll be largely your fault,' Rosa said brutally.

'But you're going to get her off. You must. That girl's lying.'

'How do you know if you were asleep?' There was no reply and she went on in an urgent tone, 'Who exactly are you and what are you up to?'

The question was blurted out almost before she realised what she had said. It had lain in her mind so long and now it had leapt out with the sudden agility of a sand-hopper.

There was a brief, fraught silence before he said in a stony voice, 'I'm Peter Atkins. Who else?' A second later he had rung off.

It was half-past seven before Rosa arrived in Worthing. As she parked outside the house, she observed the canvas shelter on the pavement. On the grass verge outside its entrance flap a saucepan of stew was steaming on the small spirit stove. Human shadows floated in grotesque relief on the wall of the shelter, making it look as if the occupants were engaged in slow-motion wrestling.

She locked her car and walked up the path to the front door.

'Sorry I'm late,' she said as Sarah let her in. 'As usual I got held up just as I was leaving the office.'

'I hope you don't mind if we eat in,' Sarah remarked as she closed the door and gave Rosa a nervously welcoming smile. 'I had planned to take you out for a meal, but I suddenly funked the thought of a public restaurant. Stupid, as nobody's going to recognise me.'

'It suits me to eat in. In fact I'd prefer it.'

'It'll just be the two of us. I've got rid of Nicole for the night. A friend who lives on a farm between here and Horsham has taken her off my hands.' With a small shiver she added, 'I particularly didn't want to have Nicole around in the morning.'

'Any further news of Peter?' Rosa enquired casually.

Sarah shook her head. 'Geoffrey Traill phoned this morning – I'm beginning to hate the sound of his voice – Anyway he said Peter was all right but felt too embarrassed to speak to me personally. *Enbarrassed*! I ask you! He ought to feel worse than that after the way he's behaved.' She gave Rosa a bewildered look. 'I'm being torn all ways. Sometimes I'm worried sick, at others I'm just angry at what he's done, and in between I sink into total apathy. Anyway, let's have a drink before we have supper.'

It was time, Rosa decided, to mention Peter's phone call to her that afternoon. When she had finished Sarah said, 'Nothing makes sense any more.' She went on in a bitter tone, 'The only thing that's clear is that Peter has more important things in his life than me and Nicole. There was a time when I'd never have believed that.'

'Obviously, Geoffrey Traill is more than a mere friend,' Rosa observed.

'As far as I'm concerned he's become a thoroughly sinister figure. Incidentally, did you notice the canvas shelter on the pavement outside?'

'Yes.'

'It was there the morning after Peter walked out. It also suddenly appeared after the awful Mr Peterson had tried to photograph us when we were leaving the house.'

'I remember your mentioning it. What are they supposed to be doing?'

'I've no idea. I tried to put my head through the flap and see what was going on, but a burly figure blocked my way. I did ask him what they were up to and he just said they were testing some new equipment. When I asked him how long they'd be there, he merely shrugged.'

'What sort of equipment?' Rosa asked with a frown.

'That's what I wondered too. I wouldn't be surprised if they don't have some electronic device in there which enables them to listen to everyone's conversations for miles around. I noticed that they had a telephone in one corner of the shelter.'

'You could always ring the police and say there are suspicious characters parked on the pavement outside your house.'

'I know, but I'm not too keen to get further involved with the police.' She gave Rosa a wan smile. 'In a curious way I've come to find them more comforting than menacing.'

As they were clearing away the dirty dishes, Rosa said, 'That was a lovely meal. Somebody else's cooking is always a treat. You must give me your recipe for boeuf stroganoff, it was absolutely delicious. The few times I've tried to make it have proved remarkably unsuccessful. And your lemon mousse had the texture of gossamer.'

Sarah turned her head away, but not before Rosa had seen a tear start to trickle down her cheek.

'Actually they're both favourites of Peter's,' she said in a wistful voice. Then picking up the coffee tray and leading the way into the living room she said, 'Why don't we go the whole hog and have a liqueur? Two females dining alone and finishing with liqueurs conjures up a splendidly decadent scene. We've got brandy, Kümmel, Drambuie and Crème de Menthe.'

'I'll have Crème de Menthe because I love the colour.'

Seated back in the living-room Sarah said, 'I suppose we ought to talk about tomorrow.'

'There's not a great deal to say, though it might be as well to remind you of the procedure. The first thing to mention is that you won't be asked to plead. That's because the magistrates are not trying the case, merely deciding whether there's sufficient evidence to justify a committal to the crown court. Prosecuting counsel will open the case and then he'll call Cheryl Peterson to give her evidence. After that the statements of all the other witnesses will be read. Finally, I shall make a submission of no case to answer and prosecuting counsel will reply, after which the magistrates will retire and consider their decision.' She paused. 'If I fail to make any impression on Cheryl Peterson,' she went on in a thoughtful tone, 'it'll be a waste of time to submit no case to answer.' Observing Sarah's anxious expression she added quickly, 'But it won't be for want of effort if I do fail to discredit her evidence. That's really it in a nutshell. I imagine we shall have to run the gauntlet of reporters and photographers outside the court, but there's nothing we can do about that. But don't be drawn into making any comment.'

'I won't even open my mouth to say good morning to anyone. Will you and the prosecuting counsel be the only two lawyers in court?'

'Somebody called Jennie Passmore will be there from the D.P.P.'s office, instructing their counsel. Also I wouldn't be surprised if there isn't someone holding a watching brief on behalf of Jonathan Cool's family.'

'What does that involve?'

141

'Sitting and listening and noting anything that reflects on Cool. Counsel with a watching brief has no right of audience and, in general, can speak only if spoken to. The magistrates can allow him to make a brief statement in open court at the end of the proceedings, but it's at their discretion.'

'One thing for sure, Peter won't be there,' Sarah remarked after a pause.

'What about Mr Jameson?' Rosa asked quickly.

'He said he'd come.' With a faint smile she added, 'I think he feels *in loco parentis*.'

It was half-past eleven before Rosa glanced at her watch and declared it her bedtime. The evening had passed more quickly than she had expected. Over a second Drambuie Sarah had talked about herself. Of how when she had reached the age of twenty-seven she had felt that marriage had passed her by, only to meet Peter a year later and fall as completely in love with him as he had with her.

'There was I twenty-eight and Peter over forty and it was as if we had both been struck by thunderbolts. It was utterly magical.'

She went on to tell Rosa that Peter had always been a very private person and that she had respected his reticence and never tried to probe his past. The present and the future were all that mattered to her, especially after Nicole had been born.

'I trusted Peter implicitly,' she said, 'and I knew that our marriage had given him something previously missing in his life.'

As Rosa got into bed, she wondered whether the next day would shed any fresh light on the mystery surrounding her client's husband. She didn't think it likely, nor even see how it could, but court proceedings had a way of illuminating the unexpected.

Chapter 21

Stan Peterson timed his and his daughter's arrival at court to maximum effect. As he guided her across the road in front of the court house he noted with satisfaction the clutch of photographers and press men gathered outside. They had already observed the approach of the star witness.

'Just relax,' he murmured for the hundredth time. 'You've nothing to worry about. Put on a bit of a smile, but don't look too happy.'

The last thing Cheryl felt at that moment was happy. She was wearing a black skirt and a white angora wool sweater with a halter neckline. Her father had ordained what she should put on and she had followed his wishes to avoid an argument. In his view black would symbolise her continuing grief and white signified virginity and spirituality, neither of which she happened to possess.

As they reached the pavement several photographers closed in and Stan put a restraining hand on her arm to slow her down. She felt tense and frightened and came near to being sick over their feet.

Once they reached the relative sanctuary of the court house, Stan hustled her into a small room and told her to wait.

'Just relax and I'll be back in a minute,' he said. 'I'd better go and find prosecuting counsel and tell him we're here. He may want to have a word with you before the case starts.'

Rosa and Sarah, for their part, arrived by taxi, Rosa having pointed out that this would obviate the problem of parking as well as exposing them less to public gaze.

Inevitably, however, photographers were on the look-out for

Sarah's arrival and the two women made a final dash for the entrance as though it had suddenly come on to rain. Sarah automatically held up a hand to shield her face from the prying cameras and immediately felt foolish. After all, it was Peter, rather than herself, who was paranoid about the possibility of being photographed.

As they entered the vestibule of the court they spotted Mr Jameson standing with his back to the wall beside the entrance to one of the court rooms. Because he still had on his ancient black homburg, he appeared to tower over everyone else. As always it sat so straight on his head that Rosa had the impression he had adjusted it with the aid of a spirit level. They pushed their way over to him. He didn't notice them, however, until they had almost reached him, when his expression relaxed and he stooped to give Sarah a kiss on the cheek. His hat was knocked askew, but he quickly re-adjusted its angle.

'Don't laugh,' he said, 'but I was taken for a barrister just before you arrived. Someone came up and asked if I was Robert Gidman. He said he'd been told to look for someone tall and I was the only person he could see who was both tall and in barrister's attire.'

Rosa laughed, but Sarah was too busy staring rigidly at his waistcoat button to react.

'Not many barristers wear black jackets and striped trousers these days,' Rosa said.

'I didn't think I'd be let inside unless I was appropriately dressed.'

'You'd still have got in if you'd come in jeans and a T-shirt.'

'Another illusion destroyed,' he remarked with a sigh. 'Life has lost enough decorum without the law yielding its standards.'

'Only its sartorial standards,' Rosa said with a self-deprecating smile. 'I don't suppose I'm dressed as you expected me to be.'

'You look utterly delightful. Though to be truthful I'd imagined you'd be in a black coat and skirt and a white blouse. The female equivalent of what I thought male barristers wore.'

Rosa laughed. 'I bet, too, you gave me a neckline that just

144

allowed my head to show. In fact, I always try and strike a balance between the drab and the frivolous when I go to court.'

'And most successfully, my dear!'

Rosa glanced down at her black woollen dress which had multi-coloured hoops in rainbow hues round its hem and was similarly trimmed at the cuffs.

'Excuse me, are you Rosa Epton?' asked a somewhat haughty voice.

She turned round to find a girl giving her an enquiring look.

'Yes.'

'I'm Jennie Passmore from the Director's department. Robert Gidman would like to have a word with you before we start. He's in court.'

'I'll be with you in a moment,' Rosa said.

So that was the person with whom the Assistant Director had thought she would be well matched. She had been wearing a well-cut grey check skirt with a burgundy red twin set. She had carefully groomed straight fair hair which reached to her shoulders. Indeed, aside from her legs, she could have been a fashion model. But her legs would easily support a billiard table, Rosa reflected agreeably.

'We'll go to the jailer's office so that you can surrender to your bail,' she said to Sarah, 'and then I'll go and see what prosecuting counsel wants.'

Robert Gidman was tall and angular. He had thinning hair and a melancholy expression. As soon as he spoke, however, his appearance was forgotten. His voice was one of the most attractive Rosa had ever heard.

'Ah, good morning, Miss Epton. I thought we ought to have a word before kick-off. Would I be right in thinking that you still wish me to call Miss Peterson?'

'Yes.'

'Very well. No other witnesses?'

'No, only her. Are any other witnesses here then?'

'Only a few police officers,' he said with an engaging smile. 'May I ask if you're likely to be calling your client at this stage?'

145

'The answer's no, I shan't be.'

'That presumably means you won't be calling any evidence at all?'

Rosa felt the question was not quite as innocent as it seemed.

'That's right,' she said.

'Good. Then it seems we're ready to start. Incidentally, I gather the deceased's family have somebody coming to hold a watching brief.' He glanced round. 'That could be him arriving now. I'll just find out.'

Rosa opened her briefcase and extracted her papers, setting them out neatly as though laying a table for dinner. This done, she turned to see if Mr Jameson had found himself a place. He was at the very back squeezed incongruously between two girls who were talking to each other across his front. He gave Rosa a tiny wave.

A minute or two later an usher called for silence and three magistrates trooped on to the bench. The Chairman was a short tubby man with a bald head and a small moustache. He wore a pair of gold-rimmed spectacles. Bank official with part-time military connections, Rosa thought to herself. He was flanked by a middle-aged female with precariously pinned-up grey hair and a much younger man whose shirt collar was clearly uncomfortably tight, to judge from the way he constantly ran a finger round the inside band.

Sarah's name was called and she came into court. The clerk said he was sure her solicitor had already explained the nature of the proceedings to her. He then read out the charge which was that on the 29th October 1982 she had caused the death of Jonathan Charles Coolie in Downland Road, Worthing, by driving a motor car recklessly having regard to all the circumstances of the case, contrary to Section 50 of the Criminal Law Act 1977.

After which he invited Sarah to sit down and Robert Gidman to stand up and present his case. At this point the representatives of the media metaphorically licked their pencils and leaned hopefully forward.

146

'I appear in this case, your worships, on behalf of the Director of Public Prosecutions and the defendant, Mrs Sarah Atkins, is represented by Miss Epton.'

Watching prosecuting counsel rise to his feet and begin addressing the bench reminded Rosa of a stiff-jointed cartoon figure going into action.

'The charge, as you've heard, is one of causing death by reckless driving,' he went on. 'If you decide that the evidence presents a prima facie case, then the prosecution will invite you to commit the defendant for trial at the crown court. The charge arises out of an accident in Downland Road at about ten-thirty on the evening of Friday 29th October last. The defendant, with her husband as a front-seat passenger in the car, was driving home from a party they had been attending at Mr Jameson's Language School in Swift Road. Mr Atkins is a teacher at the school and the occasion for the party was Mr Jameson's birthday. Following the accident the defendant, in accordance with normal procedure, was given a breathalyser test which showed her to have seven milligrammes of alcohol in her blood over the prescribed limit. That is not a large excess, but sufficient, nevertheless, for her to be charged with the relevant offence and for the prosecution to adduce evidence of it as part of their case against her on the charge with which we're concerned today. The final disposal of the breathalyser charge is a matter for another time.

'The evening of 29th October was one of patchy sea mist. In some places quite thick, in others less so. One of the denser patches was at the scene of the accident in Downland Road where visibility was around fifteen yards.

'Before describing what happened, let me say something about the deceased. His name was Jonathan Coolie, better known to the public as Jonathan Cool, and he was twenty-four years old at the time of his death. He was a pop star turned actor who had achieved considerable fame and following in the course of his short life. Rather remarkably, perhaps, he was a non-drinker, as well as being a non-smoker. Moreover, I mention it merely to dismiss it, there's never been any evidence that he was a

147

drug-taker.

'On the evening in question he had driven down to Worthing to visit his girlfriend, Miss Cheryl Peterson, who is eighteen years old and who lives with her parents in Melford Avenue. He picked her up at her home and they drove to Fables Club at Goring where they had dinner. They left just after ten o'clock with the intention of dropping Miss Peterson home, after which Mr Cool was going to drive back to London. When they reached Downland Avenue, Mr Cool parked the car in order to get out and urinate. Miss Peterson will tell you that he stopped at that particular spot because the mist would ensure him privacy and because he knew there was a small plot of waste land. Before he got out of his car, which was a Lotus, he turned on his yellow flashing hazard lights. In addition, the car was showing its red rear lights and parking lights in front.

'Miss Peterson will tell you that he was gone only a couple of minutes, during which time she remained in the car. She saw him come round the front to get back in. He was just about to open the driver's door when the accident occurred. I should have mentioned that he had parked on his correct side of the road so that the driver's door was on the opposite side to the kerb. There is evidence, indeed, that the car could not have been parked closer to its nearside kerb than it was. According to Miss Peterson the defendant's car came out of the mist from behind at a speed that was clearly reckless in these conditions and struck Mr Cool as he stood beside the door of his car. As a result he was hurled forward on to the road and sustained severe head injuries from which he died before reaching hospital.'

Mr Gidman gave the magistrates a long, sorrowful look. Rosa had found his voice mesmerising even when reciting prosaic facts. It would be wonderful, she reflected, to have him read to you when you were tucked up ill in bed.

'As your worships will know,' Gidman now continued, 'it is not uncommon in cases of this nature to have a wealth of technical evidence relating to skid marks and braking power and matters of that sort. The prosecution in this case, however, have no such data

148

to lead. The deceased's car was, of course, stationary at the time. Nevertheless it was thoroughly examined afterwards and found to have no mechanical defects. In particular all its lights were in good working order. The defendant's Toyota Tercel was also found to be in excellent mechanical condition, with, I should stress, nothing whatsoever at fault with its brakes. It had suffered damage to its nearside front wing where it had struck Mr Cool and hurled him forward.

'Apart from a short skid mark indicating the point at which the defendant had suddenly applied her brakes there is no circumstantial evidence to show the exact path of her car immediately prior to the accident. Morever, there were no independent witnesses to what happened. Despite intensive police enquiries nobody has come forward to give any information which could help you. Nobody appears to have seen the Lotus during the short time it was parked at the roadside, nor to have witnessed the approach of the defendant's car.' He leaned forward slightly, resting his fingertips on the ledge in front of him. 'The prosecution's case,' he intoned solemnly, 'rests on the evidence of Miss Cheryl Peterson who was in the parked Lotus when it all happened. If you accept what she says, then there can be no doubt that Mr Cool lost his life because the defendant was driving recklessly, given the road conditions. If Mrs Atkins had been driving with proper care, there seems to have been no earthly reason why she shouldn't have seen the Lotus and had time to take avoiding action. One reason, of course, may well have been because her driving ability had been impaired by alcohol. Her reactions, so vital in these adverse conditions, were slower and less positive than they might otherwise have been.'

As Rosa listened she reflected that prosecutors were never more deadly than when adopting a soft approach. Robert Gidman managed to produce a soothing sound even when clearing his throat.

'At the police station,' he went on, 'Mrs Atkins elected to make a statement giving her own version of what took place. I have to tell you that it conflicts in every vital detail with the account

149

given by Miss Peterson, in particular as to the lights on the parked Lotus. According to the defendant it was not displaying any lights at all; in fact, it was parked at the kerbside in total darkness.' Prosecuting counsel gave the bench a searching look. 'Unfortunately, Miss Peterson and Mrs Atkins can't both be right. Though it's not for me to speculate, it may be that the shock of the accident somehow caused the defendant to imagine afterwards that the Lotus had been parked in darkness. At all events, there's no doubt that the lights referred to by Miss Peterson were showing when people arrived on the scene shortly afterwards.

'Let me say that Mrs Atkins is a person of unblemished character, as was Mr Cool. This was a tragic accident in which a young man of outstanding promise and talent was killed. Sentiment, however, has no part in the criminal law and you must be guided solely by the evidence. Mrs Atkins is not being prosecuted because she knocked down and killed a widely known and popular public figure, but because she drove her car in a reckless manner and thereby caused an innocent person's death.'

As prosecuting counsel reached the end of his speech, Stan Peterson hurried out of court. He had been perched uninvited at the end of a row of Press men and had been following events with frowning disapproval. Before the case had begun he had introduced himself to counsel as 'one of your colleagues in the other branch' and as the father of his coming star witness. Gidman had been warned that Cheryl Peterson's father was a clerk in a solicitor's office who gave himself professional airs and graces. Accordingly, he reacted coolly to the greeting and rejected the suggestion that he might like to speak to Cheryl before proceedings started. Stan had not taken kindly to the rebuff and had been in no frame of mind to approve the low-key note on which counsel opened his case. In his, Stan's view, the prosecution ought to go on the offensive from the outset; in particular, Cheryl's evidence should have been referred to in a much more partisan spirit. When, towards the end of his opening, Gidman had said to the court that Cheryl and the defendant

150

couldn't both be right about the car lights, Stan had almost bubbled over with indignation. Of course they couldn't be, but counsel had needed to be much more aggressive in pointing out why it was Cheryl's evidence which should be believed.

When he emerged from court, he found his daughter sitting alone on a bench.

'You'll be on any moment,' he said hurriedly. 'You've nothing to worry about, so relax. Think of Jonathan and tell the court exactly what happened that evening. . . how her car came charging out of the mist and mowed him down. . .'

The usher chose this moment to come to the court room door and call out Cheryl's name. Her father put out a helping hand, but she brushed it aside and stalked ahead of him into court. Rosa, who had swivelled round in her seat to observe her entry, noted her father's presence immediately behind. She wondered whether he had been giving his daughter last-minute advice.

Cheryl took the oath in a whisper and lowered her gaze to somewhere on the court room floor.

'Is your name Cheryl Peterson?' Gidman asked.

'Yes.'

'Where do you live, Miss Peterson?'

'Eight Melford Avenue.'

He had deliberately not asked the question in a leading form as he hoped that by getting her to answer preliminary, uncontroversial questions she would slowly feel more at ease.

'How old are you?'

'Eighteen.'

'You must speak up, Miss Peterson,' the Chairman said a trifle testily. 'We've all got to hear your evidence.'

'And what's your occupation?' counsel went on.

'I work in a beauty salon.'

'Didn't hear a word of that,' the Chairman grumbled.

'She says she works in a beauty salon, your worship.'

'Oh!' In an audible aside to his female colleague on the bench, the Chairman observed, 'Pity it's not with an elocutionist.'

At this point the clerk of the court rose and whispered something

151

to the Chairman, who said, 'If she sits down, we'll hear even less.' He glanced towards the witness. 'Do you want to have a chair?'

'No, I'm all right,' Cheryl replied with a note of undisguised hostility. She was aware that her father was watching her intently, but she refused to look in his direction.

'How long had you known Jonathan Cool?' counsel now asked.

'Three months.'

'Would you see each other quite often?'

'Yes, he used to spend all his spare time with me.'

'How would you describe your relationship?'

'He was in love with me.'

'And what were your feelings towards him?'

'I quite liked him.'

Stan Peterson stared at his daughter in disbelief, but she still disdained to look at him.

Robert Gidman stared thoughtfully at the statement he was holding – the statement in which Cheryl had spoken of their undying love for one another. On balance he decided not to press the matter as the exact nature of their relationship was of only peripheral relevance. But it was always disquieting when a witness began to depart from his or her proof of evidence. It was like being on quicksands. In his succeeding questions he elicited details of their evening together before the accident took place.

'While you were in Fables did Mr Cool have anything to drink?'

'Yes, Coca-Cola.'

'Was that all?'

'Yes.'

'No alcohol?'

'He never touched alcohol.'

'What did you have to drink?'

'I had a vodka and lime before dinner and a Pimms Number One with the meal.'

'Anything else?'

'No.'

'Did what you had affect you?'

152

'I wasn't drunk if that's what you mean.'

It was apparent that the witness was becoming more assured with every answer she gave. When she had first entered the box, she had looked so forlorn and vulnerable that Sarah had felt almost sorry for her. It was hard to believe that a pretty young girl could be prepared to destroy somebody's life with such cold calculation. But the prettiness was that of a stereotype and nothing could mask the fundamental selfishness that lay beneath. As Sarah was thinking this the girl gave her a sudden look. It was a look that conveyed absolutely nothing, however; neither hatred nor fear, nor even a note of imminent triumph. It made Sarah yearn to see inside her head. What was going on beneath those blonde curls?

A few more questions from prosecuting counsel brought her to the time and place of the accident.

'What happened when you reached Downland Avenue?' he asked.

'Jonathan stopped the car and got out.'

'For what purpose?'

'It's in my statement.'

'I know it is, Miss Peterson, but I must still ask you to tell the court. Don't be embarrassed!'

'He wanted to have a piss,' she said with a slight snigger.

'Did you stay in the car?'

'Yes.'

'What lights was the car showing when he left it?' The question was accompanied by a stern, compelling look.

'He switched on the hazard lights before he got out.'

'Are those yellow, flashing lights?'

'Yes.'

'What about other lights?'

'We'd been driving on dipped headlights and he turned them off, leaving just the parking lights on.'

'What about rear lights?'

'I didn't get out to see,' she replied almost pertly, before adding, 'But I'd seen them reflected in a window on our way

153

back.'

'How long was Mr Cool gone?'

'About a couple of minutes.'

'Were you able to see him while he was away from the car?'

'I didn't try to. Anyway the mist hid him.'

'What happened next?'

'He suddenly appeared in front of the car and came round to get in.'

'How thick was the mist at that time?'

She gave a shrug. 'About the same, I think. I didn't give it any particular attention.'

'What was the next thing?'

'I suddenly heard this car with its engine racing coming up behind and there was a terrific thud as it hit Jonathan.' Her lips started to tremble and she reached out for the glass of water on the ledge in front of her and took a sip.

'I realise this is very distressing for you, Miss Peterson,' Gidman said, 'and I'll try not to prolong your ordeal.'

To Rosa, there was a fine distinction between putting the witness at ease and stirring her emotions. However, the words were out and beyond recall and any protest would, she felt, be a psychological error.

'How close to his own car was he standing when the other car hit him?'

'He was right beside it and had his hand on the door to open it.'

'What did you do after he'd been struck?'

'I think I must have fainted for a few seconds. I remember seeing people moving about in the mist.'

'Did you get out of the car?'

'I believe so, though I don't recall anything very clearly. I think I went to where he was lying in the road, but I don't really remember.'

'Did you notice the driver of the other car?'

'No. I've been told I screamed at her that she'd killed Jonathan, but I have no recollection of doing so.'

Gidman had only a few further questions before resuming his seat. He felt his witness had given her evidence in a reasonably convincing manner and had come up to proof on the essentials. He doubted whether Rosa would make much effect on her in cross-examination.

Stan Peterson, for his part, was trying everything short of double somersaults to attract his daughter's gaze, but she still steadfastly refused to look in his direction. He had been shocked by the way she had described her relationship with Jonathan, but thereafter there had been no further anxious moments. Having failed to get Cheryl's attention he turned and glared at Rosa as she came to her feet, scooping back her hair which had a habit of falling forward on either side of her face.

'Can you drive a car, Miss Peterson?' she asked, causing the witness to falter at the unexpectedness of the question.

'Yes.'

'Have you passed your driving test or do you hold only a provisional licence?'

'I've passed my test.'

'Do you enjoy driving?'

'Yes.'

'Do you have a car of your own?'

'No.'

'Did you ever drive Mr Cool's Lotus?'

'He let me do so a few times. But only short distances.'

'You must have particularly enjoyed driving a car of that class?'

'Yes.'

'Did you ever drive it at night?'

'No.'

'But you were frequently a passenger after dark?'

'Yes.' Her tone was puzzled and suspicious.

'May I take it then, Miss Peterson, that you knew how to switch on the lights?'

The witness gave Rosa an angry look.

'Of course I did,' she said in a taut voice. 'But if you're

155

suggesting I switched them on after the accident, it's a lie. They were on all the time.'

'Which were on all the time?' Rosa asked calmly.

'I've already explained. Jonathan turned on the hazard lights before he got out. The others were on, as I've said.'

'Do you think you could be mistaken?'

'Definitely not.'

'Is it possible you switched on the lights yourself after the accident as a sort of automatic reflex to what happened?'

'I told you, I fainted for a few seconds,' Cheryl said defiantly, while her father directed a furious stare at Rosa.

'It wouldn't have taken more than a second to turn on the lights. After all, you've admitted you were familiar with the switches.'

'Well, I didn't. I'm not the one who's lying,' she said with a touch of viciousness.

'Don't excite yourself,' the Chairman interrupted. 'The defendant's solicitor is only doing her duty.'

For a moment it seemed that Cheryl was about to tell him what he could do with his interventions. Meanwhile, Rosa was reflecting that she had a tougher nut to crack than she had bargained for. She hadn't expected the witness to collapse at the first question, but it was now apparent that Cheryl Peterson was ready to brazen out her original lie and even fortify her position with further lies when necessary. Rosa had somehow not been prepared for such barefaced perjury even though she had been practising the criminal law long enough to know how deceptive appearances could be. Villainous faces could conceal hearts of gold, and, by contrast, a pretty one could cloak a mind full of wicked intention. But was she going to be able to demonstrate to the court just how unscrupulous a liar the witness was?

'In your statement to the police made immediately after the accident, Miss Peterson, you describe your relationship with Jonathan Cool very differently from what you've told the court today. Where lies the truth?'

Cheryl bit nervously at her lower lip before replying.

156

'I've had time to think,' she said, staring down at the floor. 'I suppose I was rather swept off my feet by Jonathan. I was flattered by his attention and thought I was in love with him when I wasn't really.' She gave a small shrug as if to indicate that summed it up.

'In your statement you say you were crazily in love with one another. Am I to take it that wasn't true so far as your own feelings were concerned?'

'I thought it was true at the time,' she said with a note of defiance.

'Did you not also tell the press that you were deeply in love with each other?'

'What if I did? Anyway it was my dad who kept on pushing me to say things like that.'

'So the truth is that you quite liked him, to quote your words today, but nothing more?'

'Yes, we had some good times together.' She paused. 'As Jonathan Cool's girlfriend I had an image to live up to,' she added, as though that explained everything.

'So what you said in your statement wasn't true?'

'It wasn't a lie either, because I thought it was true when I said it.'

'You were merely living up to the image you've referred to?'

'Yes,' she said with a satisfied nod.

'And were quite prepared to lie for that purpose?'

'I've told you it wasn't a lie,' she retorted crossly.

However nervous she had been when she began her evidence, it was now apparent that no amount of cross-examination was going to bring about her sudden collapse. It was turning into a war of attrition.

'Are you somebody who readily lies?' Rosa asked.

'No more than most people.'

'Does that mean you lie when it suits your purpose?'

'Everyone does.'

'Never mind everyone. You do, is that right?'

'Haven't you ever told lies?' Cheryl replied scathingly.

157

Rosa ignored the question and went on quickly. 'What's the difference between lying about your relationship with Jonathan and lying about the lights on his car?'

'There is a difference, that's all.'

'Describe it.'

'I can't. It's obvious.'

'Is that the best answer you can give?'

'Yes.'

'Are you prepared to lie to help others as well as yourself?'

'I don't go round telling lies all the time,' she said indignantly.

'I didn't suggest you did. All I'm trying to do is establish the frontiers of your lying. Would you have lied to help Jonathan?'

'I might have done.'

'The more so when you believed you were in love with him?'

'I expect so,' she said off-handedly, then added quickly, 'But I'm not lying about the car lights. That's what you're trying to get me to say, isn't it?'

'*Supposing* Jonathan had left the car in darkness, would you have been prepared to switch them on to get him out of trouble?'

'I didn't have to because he did switch them on.' The reply came back like a hard-hit squash ball off the front wall.

'But *supposing* he hadn't. . .?

'Yes, I would, because it wouldn't make me a liar, would it?'

'That would depend on what you told anyone afterwards.'

'You're trying to confuse me. Anyway, it didn't happen like that.'

'May I take it that you wouldn't want to have seen Jonathan in trouble?'

'What trouble?'

'Trouble with the police.'

' 'Course I wouldn't.'

'You'd have been prepared to cover up for him?'

'Yes, but I never had to.' She threw Rosa a quietly triumphant look.

Rosa remained in thought for a moment and then abruptly sat down. She had extracted admissions that might count with a

158

jury, but which were less likely to carry weight with a bench of magistrates deciding a different issue. She turned and gave Sarah a small smile.

Robert Gidman had, meanwhile, risen to his feet to re-examine the witness.

'It has been suggested with great persistence, Miss Peterson, that you have lied to the court about the lights on Mr Cool's car. Have you done so?'

'No.'

'So what you've told the court today is the truth?'

'Yes.'

'Thank you, Miss Peterson,' he said and sat down again.

Cheryl blinked in a dazed manner and then suddenly crumpled in a dead faint. Her father and the usher reached her together and lifted her on to a chair. After a few sips of water she was assisted to her feet, looking as white as her angora wool sweater. Meanwhile a woman police officer hurried forward with smelling salts.

'Let her go and sit outside,' the clerk said. 'She can sign her deposition later.'

'It was the strain,' Stan Peterson said, casting an accusing glance round the court. He seemed to be addressing nobody in particular and nobody responded.

Rosa watched thoughtfully as the witness was assisted from court. She had known witnesses to faint before now, but never at the end of their evidence. It could only have been the sudden release of tension that her ordeal was over. It would have suited Rosa better if she had fainted earlier.

For the next twenty minutes the statements of other prosecution witnesses were read out. Then Cheryl was called back into court and the clerk read her deposition to her and she signed it. She looked as pale as an aspirin and as if in a kind of trance. When her father tried to stand just behind her, he was told politely, but firmly, to move right away. Rosa's original assumption that the girl was completely under her father's domination had been somewhat contradicted by her evidence.

Gidman now said that on the evidence he'd adduced he sought

159

a committal for trial at the crown court.

Rosa had always liked to think that she didn't waste a court's time by making submissions of no case to answer which had no chance of succeeding. In the present instance, however, she knew she had boxed herself in. Not to make a submission would be an admission of her failure to discredit Cheryl Peterson's evidence. Furthermore, she knew that Sarah was expecting her to fight to the bitter end. Worse still, she suspected her client's hopes were greater than her own.

Accordingly, she now rose dutifully to her feet and began.

'I submit, your worships, that you ought not to commit the defendant for trial on the available evidence. It is not evidence upon which a jury acting reasonably could possibly convict. I refer, of course, to the testimony of Miss Peterson on which the prosecution's case is founded. She is a self-confessed liar who frankly admits to being someone to whom telling the truth is little more than a matter of personal convenience. You may have thought that her answers to vital questions were, at times, frighteningly glib and far from the sort of evidence on which a prosecution ought to rely. . .

'On the issue of what lights, if any, the Lotus was showing at the time of the accident, you're entitled to have regard to what the defendant has said in her written statement. The prosecution has adduced it as part of their case and they can't pick and choose which bits of it they'd like you to rely on and which bits to ignore. It must be considered as a whole. . .'

Rosa was gratified to observe that the bench was listening to her with concentrated attention, though the young man on the Chairman's left still seemed to be suffering from mild strangulation by his shirt collar.

'I would urge you,' she now went on, 'not to be influenced by the publicity this unhappy case has attracted. The defence don't dispute that Jonathan Cool was a highly talented young actor with a glowing future before him. That makes his death all the more tragic, but it doesn't mean that somebody must therefore pay a penalty for what happened. You shouldn't apply different

160

standards in assessing the evidence in this case than you would had the victim been someone wholly unknown to the public. I know you wouldn't consciously do so, but the subconscious pressure is there and must be recognised and rejected. . . .'

A few moments later she reached the end of her submission. 'I ask you to dismiss this charge on the grounds that no jury acting reasonably could possibly convict on the evidence the prosecution has put before you.'

The Chairman gave her a brisk nod as she sat down.

Prosecuting counsel rose to his feet like a stiff-jointedly daddy-long-legs. Then his silvery voice took over and his odd appearance was forgotten.

After pouring gentle reproof on what Rosa had said about his chief witness he went on, 'You, on the other hand, may think she was a most truthful person. She didn't pretend to be purer than driven snow and never to tell an untruth, but even under the most penetrating cross-examination she remained unshaken on the question of the car lights. Moreover, is it likely that in the split second aftermath of this ghastly accident she would have had the cool presence of mind to lean across and switch on all those lights?'

The question seemed to hang in the air for all to consider before being answered with a resounding negative.

He said that only a cold-blooded monster could have told such a wicked lie and perpetuated it from that day to this. . . . 'In any event,' he concluded, 'this was surely an issue for a jury, and not examining magistrates, to decide.'

A hoarse bark from the usher brought everyone to their feet, as the magistrates, clutching sheaves of notes, disappeared through a door at the back of their dais. Robert Gidman was claimed in earnest conversation by Jennie Passmore and Rosa went to have a word with Sarah who was sitting forlornly in the dock. She gave Rosa a pallid smile.

'How long before they reach a decision?' she asked nervously.

'Long enough to satisfy the niceties,' Rosa replied ruefully. 'I think you must be prepared for a committal. I'm afraid Cheryl

Peterson was a tougher proposition than I'd hoped for.'

'But she was lying. Anyone could tell she was lying. How could they possibly believe her?'

Rosa sighed. 'The trouble is they're not trying the case; they don't have to decide where the truth lies, only whether there's evidence on which a jury could convict.'

'But no jury could possibly convict,' Sarah exclaimed in anguish.

'It could if it accepted her evidence,' Rosa said bleakly.

Sarah shook her head disbelievingly as though her life had been caught in a sudden squall and was finally about to capsize.

Rosa realised that it was bad enough for a respectable woman to be facing trial in the crown court on a criminal charge, but to have this happen when your husband has deserted you in the most mysterious of circumstances was more than anyone deserved. As she gave Sarah a quick glance, she felt a sharp stab in her own heart. Although she had tried not to give her client false hopes, she couldn't help feeling a measure of responsibility for her crushed appearance. She didn't expect to win all her cases, but this was one in which her own private hopes had been pitched higher than events justified. She had persuaded herself that if Cheryl Peterson really was a perjurer, it should be possible to expose this to the court. Perhaps she'd expected her perjury to be half-hearted and apologetic, instead of which it had been brazen and utterly assured.

When a few minutes later the magistrates returned to the bench and announced to a packed court that they considered the defendant did have a case to answer, Rosa's mind was already on the trial ahead.

Sarah's bail was renewed and Mr Jameson came up beside them as they made their way out of court. He took Sarah's hand and gave it an affectionate squeeze.

They were about to push their way outside when Sergeant Hibbert suddenly appeared.

'If you'd like to hang on for a minute, Mrs Atkins, I can give you a lift. I've got my car parked at the back. It'll save you aggro

162

from the press men out front.'

'That would be very kind,' Rosa said quickly. She had a glimpse of Stan Peterson talking to a number of newspapermen out on the forecourt. His daughter stood aloof a few paces away. When her father addressed some remark to her, she turned an eloquent shoulder on him. As Rosa watched her from the other side of the heavy glass doors, she wondered anew how to get her off the hook on which Cheryl had firmly impaled herself. Her perjury, if ever proved, would certainly earn her a prison sentence, which made it the more difficult for her to renege. Rosa found she both wanted to throw her a lifeline and grind her into small pieces.

'Are you sure you can spare the time to do this?' Rosa said, as they got into Sergeant Hibbert's car. When Sarah got into the back, Rosa automatically took the front passenger seat. She was always affronted if her own passengers sat in the rear, leaving her alone in front like a chauffeur.

'Another twenty minutes away from duty won't matter here nor there,' he remarked.

He enquired after Sarah's daughter and went on to tell them that he had a son, Tom, aged five, and a daughter, Victoria, who was three, and that his wife was expecting their third child on Christmas Eve.

'I'm lucky to have an unmarried sister-in-law who rallies round on these occasions, but I enjoy doing as much as possible myself.' With a note of quiet pride, he said, 'I've promised to take the two kids to a toy fair this Saturday and I bet I enjoy it as much as they do. People oughtn't to have children unless they're prepared to give them a fair share of their time.'

'You sound like a model father,' Rosa remarked.

'Tom doesn't think so when I bawl him out. He's a real little mischief-maker,' he said with a pleased grin.

Ten minutes later they pulled up outside the Atkins' house and he jumped out to open the doors. Rosa mentally awarded him full marks for friendliness and tact. He had avoided all mention of the case and, more curiously, perhaps, had failed to make any

163

enquiry after Sarah's husband.

As Sarah got out, she pointed at the striped canvas shelter that was still on the wide grass verge outside the house and which now appeared to be deserted. At all events, it was securely fastened in front and there was no sign of tea-making.

'Do you know anything about that?' she asked a trifle belligerently.

'A branch of Telecom,' Sergeant Hibbert said after a cursory inspection.

'They've been there on and off for over a week,' she said in an accusing tone.

Sergeant Hibbert gave her a look of mild surprise. 'I expect they know what they're up to,' he said.

'I wondered if they might be criminals.'

Sergeant Hibbert looked startled. 'I'm sure they're harmless,' he said, after a pause, 'but I'll make an enquiry when I get back and let you know.'

He opened the front gate and stood aside to let the two women through.

'Won't you come in for a cup of something?' Sarah asked with a tired smile. 'It was most kind of you to bring us back.'

'No, I won't come in, thank you, Mrs Atkins. Somebody's sure to be yelling for me even though I did tell the station where I was going.' He seemed to hesitate for a moment, then said in an embarrassed voice, 'I know you're having a rough time, Mrs Atkins, but I'm sure you'll pull through.'

Sarah blinked at him in surprise before exclaiming vehemently, '*You* don't believe that girl's telling the truth, do you? *You* know she's lying, don't you?'

He stopped and turned with his hand on the gate and met Sarah's fierce stare.

'Perjury's the commonest crime in the calendar,' he remarked. 'There's scarcely a case in which it doesn't crop up.' He gave her a small disarming smile and went on, 'Nine out of ten defendants commit perjury. It's almost expected of them and courts make allowance for it. Sometimes police officers lie in the witness box to bolster a weak case, which is much more villainous, even

164

though they persuade themselves they're doing it in a good cause, namely to ensure the conviction of a wrongdoer. Then there are those who get stuck with a lie and haven't the courage to back down. In my experience very few people admit to perjury once they've embarked on it. They even end up believing their lie to be the truth. For example, the motorist who crosses the lights at amber has convinced himself by the time he gets to court that they were still green.' He let out a long sigh as if weighed down by a lifetime of perjury in various forms. 'Miss Peterson's only eighteen and she's been under all sorts of pressure since the accident. And her father's no help to her either.'

'That's no comfort to me if a jury believes her lies,' Sarah burst out.

'I realise that,' he said with a slightly helpless shrug. 'I've never been one of those who pretend our system of justice is perfect. Only some of the judges with their heads in the legal clouds believe that.'

'Can't you try and get her to admit she's lying?' Sarah asked in an imploring tone.

He shook his head. 'She's now a witness bound over to attend the trial. Miss Epton would be the first to protest if the police went round re-interviewing prosecution witnesses at this stage.'

Rosa smiled. 'If you can get Cheryl Peterson to admit she's told lies, you'll have my blessing.'

'I've been talking out of turn,' he said with a self-deprecating gesture, 'and now I really must be on my way.'

'I wish all police officers were as pleasant and helpful,' Rosa remarked as they went indoors.

Sarah, however, was in no mood to endorse the accolade and Rosa couldn't really blame her.

An hour later as she drove back to London, Rosa was still pondering how to crack Cheryl Peterson's evidence. She saw herself as a sharp-billed sea-bird confronted by a particularly resistant mollusc. There had to be a way of getting inside; it was all a matter of patience, plus trial and error. Endless banging at the outer shell was obviously not sufficient.

Events, however, were shortly destined to take an abrupt turn.

Chapter 22

'I don't know what's got into the girl,' Stan Peterson said crossly to his wife as he walked into the kitchen on his return home from court.

Cheryl had refused to talk on the drive back and had gone straight up to her room and firmly closed the door.

'Telling the world she was never really in love with Jonathan and only thought she was,' he went on in an indignant voice. 'If you ask me she was just being perverse. Cutting off her nose to spite her face. She's been acting strange for some time. It seems that girls in this day and age don't have proper respect for their elders and betters.'

Joan Peterson, who had listened in silence, now said, 'Why don't you tell me everything that happened, Stan?' She knew that he liked to be coaxed when he was in one of his affronted moods.

He sat down at the kitchen table and she poured him a cup of tea. While he talked, she continued with her ironing.

'The poor child's been under a terrible strain,' she remarked when he reached the end of his recital of events.

'What about me? How do you think I've felt?'

'I know, dear, but it's been even worse for Cheryl. No wonder she fainted when it was all over. It was nature's way of relieving her of tension.'

'And then not speaking as we drove home,' he continued, like a volcano deciding on another tiny eruption. 'Just stared out of the window as if I was a stranger.'

'She must have said something,' Joan remarked in a puzzled tone.

'As we set off she said, "I don't want to talk about what's

happened, dad, so please don't get at me." And when I tried to mention her evidence, she turned away from me and stared out of the window. And you heard the way she came into the house and went straight upstairs. Didn't even have a word for her mother!'

'That doesn't matter. I'm not hurt.'

'Well, I am. I could have sold her story to the press for quite a tidy sum if she'd given her evidence in a proper manner. I'd already got some offers lined up. But who'd be interested now after what she's said? There's no romance left to write about. I just don't understand what's come over her. I can tell you one thing,' he added vehemently, 'she's let me down with a bump.'

'I'm sure she never intended that,' his wife said soothingly. 'You must make more allowance.'

'After all we've done for her, too!' he said in a final indignant grumble.

Joan put down her iron, poured her husband another cup of tea and said, 'I'll go up and have a word with her.'

'If she won't talk to me, she's not likely to talk to you.'

His wife sensibly refrained from comment and moved towards the door.

'There was no sign of Atkins in court,' he said at her departing back. 'Obviously didn't dare show his face after his assault on me. He's just a common hooligan.'

His wife again decided that anything she said would only be likely to add fuel to his mood of resentment.

On reaching upstairs she listened intently outside her daughter's bedroom door before knocking.

'Yes?' Cheryl's voice sounded small and remote.

'It's me. May I come in?'

'If you want to.'

She opened the door and peered inside. Cheryl was sitting hunched on the end of her bed staring at the floor between her feet.

'How are you feeling, darling?' her mother asked in a sympathetic voice. 'Let me go down and fetch you something.' Cheryl shook her head and her mother stepped inside the room, closing the door behind her. 'My poor darling, what a terrible

167

day you've had,' she said, feeling suddenly overwhelmed with anguish at the forlorn sight on the bed. 'It must have been ghastly for you.'

'Has dad told you?'

'About your evidence? Yes, but don't let that worry you. If you didn't really love Jonathan you were right to say so. I don't blame you.'

'It was all dad's fault,' Cheryl exclaimed bitterly. 'If he hadn't kept on at me so much, I'd never have been pushed into pretending I loved Jonathan.'

Joan thought this might be a trifle unfair on her husband but didn't feel inclined to say so, particularly as she realised her daughter was close to tears. She went across and sat down beside her, putting both her arms round her in a gesture of loving protection.

'My poor, poor Cheryl,' she murmured softly with a lump in her throat.

The next moment Cheryl had buried her face in her mother's lap and was uncontrollably sobbing, while Joan stroked her hair and made soothing noises.

'What am I going to do, mum?' she gasped through her tears. 'Everything's such a mess.'

Joan Peterson was silent for a moment. 'What in particular is troubling you?' she asked gently. The response was a fresh outburst of sobbing so that she pulled her daughter to her side and held her tight. 'What is it, darling? You can tell me.'

'I just don't know what I'm going to do, mum,' she said in an exhausted whisper. 'I wish I were dead.'

'It can't be as bad as that.'

'It is. It's worse. Dad would kill me.'

'Dad doesn't have to know. It could be something just between you and me. You'll feel better if you talk about it. Bottling things up always makes them seem worse.' She gave her daughter a further quick hug. 'You always used to tell me your troubles when you were little and then you grew out of doing it, but I'm still here and still the same mum. Put me to the test and see!'

'I've told lies in court,' Cheryl said in a tight voice.

'You're certainly not the first person to do that,' her mother said robustly.

'I did turn on the lights in Jonathan's car,' she said with a note of defiance. 'He switched them all off when he got out as he didn't want anyone to come and see what was happening. He said it would be embarrassing for Jonathan Cool to be found peeing at the roadside. When the other car hit him, I quickly turned on the lights as I didn't want him to get into trouble. It was sort of automatic. I didn't think I was doing anything wrong. . .'

'And you only did it to help him,' her mother said comfortingly.

'And then when he was dead and the police asked about the lights, I felt I had to say they'd been on all the time. I was so frightened, mum. I didn't do it deliberately to get the other driver into trouble. It just sort of happened and then today the defending lawyer accused me of lying and I had to stick up for myself. I couldn't suddenly admit what I'd done in front of a whole court. And with dad sitting staring at me.'

'I understand, darling,' her mother said in a choked voice.

'Promise me you won't tell dad!'

'I'll have to think what we're going to do. Meanwhile I shan't tell him anything.'

Joan Peterson was at the same time thankful that her daughter had unburdened herself and appalled by what she had heard. She knew enough about the case to appreciate the importance of any evidence concerning the car lights. For the moment her mind was a blank as to what she ought to do. Her prime instinct was to protect her daughter, at all costs; on the other hand she knew she had a wider duty in the matter. Fortunately, there was no immediate urgency.

She heard footsteps on the stairs and the bedroom door was flung open.

'What's going on?' Stan asked in an accusing voice.

'Cheryl and I are just having a talk. I'll be down in a minute.'

'Is she all right?' Stan said nodding at his daughter who steadfastly declined to look in his direction.

'Yes.'

For half a minute he hovered in the doorway, suspicious that he was being excluded from something. Then in response to his wife's unyielding gaze, he turned and went back downstairs.

'I'd better get down,' Joan said with a sigh a little later. She gave her daughter's shoulder a squeeze. 'I'm glad you've told me, darling. It's now my problem. I'll bring you something to eat up here, if you'd sooner not come down. Meanwhile, I suggest you have a lovely hot bath. It'll help relax you.'

Stan was staring forbiddingly out of the kitchen window when she got downstairs.

'What were you and Cheryl talking about all that time?' he asked.

'I was helping her unwind. The poor child's been under an intolerable strain and today was the climax.'

'Did she say anything about the case?'

'Not really; and I suggest you don't either,' his wife said in an unusually firm voice.

Chapter 23

Soon after Rosa had departed for London, Sarah phoned her friend who was looking after Nicole and was relieved when she suggested her daughter should stay there another night.

'She's the only person Ben plays with peaceably,' Maggie said. 'I think he's probably fallen in love. I'm coming into Worthing tomorrow morning and can drop Nicole off around ten o'clock if that's all right. It'll give you a bit longer to get over today.'

Much as she adored her daughter, Sarah had not been looking forward to having her home that evening. She would certainly have proved to be a distraction, but Sarah didn't wish to be distracted. She just wanted to be alone, to think and to do whatever she wanted, without having to bother about anyone else. She even considered taking the telephone off the hook but was deterred by the thought that Peter might try and call her. She was sure he'd have found out the result of the case. Her feelings towards him were still subject to violent swings, but the day's ordeal had left her longing to hear from him. She had secretly hoped to find him in the house when Sergeant Hibbert drove her home.

Her heart skipped a beat when the phone rang. It was Mr Jameson.

'I thought I'd just call and see how you were, my dear,' he said gravely.

'As well as can be expected, as they say in hospital bulletins,' she replied with a nervous laugh.

'No news of Peter?'

'No.'

'What on earth can he be up to? It's so completely out of

character.'

'My head spins with theories, but none of them fit the Peter I know,' Sarah said wearily. 'But then how well do any of us know each other?'

'He's obviously trying to hide something in his background,' Mr Jameson went on. 'My belief is that it's to do with intelligence work.'

'As long as he's not a bank robber on the run, I don't mind.'

'I'm sure it's nothing like that.'

'I'm sure of nothing, Jamie.'

'There must be something we can do to find out.'

'You've already tried.'

'And made something of a fool of myself. I wonder what would happen if you were to get in touch with the security service and give them some sort of ultimatum. Supposing you said you were going to give your whole story to the press unless. . .'

'What story?' Sarah broke in. 'I don't have one and if the security service knows anything about Peter, they're not going to tell me.'

'But you might be able to force them into saying something.'

'I might if I had any leverage, but I haven't. They'd just file my letter in the waste-paper basket. Anyway I daren't do anything which might jeopardise Peter and as I don't know what he's up to, it means I can't do anything at all.'

Mr Jameson let out a gusty sigh. 'I wish I could be more help,' he remarked.

'I doubt whether anyone can help me. I must just await events, though that's not as easy as it sounds.'

'I realise that. You're undergoing the greatest test of faith anyone could have.'

'Faith that the husband I love turns out to be on the side of the angels and not working for the opposition, you mean?'

'I suppose that's what I do mean,' he remarked.

He himself was now convinced that Peter was involved in some intelligence activity. Moreover, he regarded it as more than a coincidence that he had sought employment in a language school where he was in contact with foreign students. It was not a thought that pleased him, even though there had never been any sort of hint that Peter had used his position for subversive ends. Nevertheless it was repugnant to him that his school might have been put to such use, under his nose and without his knowledge.

After her conversation with Mr Jameson, Sarah went and sat down in the living-room. It was dark outside and she drew the curtains, but didn't turn on any lights. The electric fire cast an agreeable, if artificial, glow and gave the room a warm look. For the umpteenth time she fell to pondering her marriage to Peter and wondering whether many women knew as little about their husbands' backgrounds as she did about hers. It had never seemed to matter before, but now it dominated her thoughts. She found herself both longing for a resumption of their life together and filled with apprehension at the prospect. Nothing could be the same again and it was a question of how much that was going to matter. Things could change and be better. . .

She felt her eyes closing and decided to surrender to sleep. When she woke up, she was cold and groped her way to the kitchen, trying to decide whether or not she was hungry. It was only eight o'clock, but she had slept for over two hours and felt totally drained of strength. Bed was the only place she wanted to be. She made a mug of hot chocolate and took it upstairs to drink while she undressed. As she got into bed she tried to ignore the cold, unoccupied half next to her.

Rather surprisingly sleep came quickly, but then something woke her up. For a moment she couldn't think what it was, until she heard voices outside. A muffled altercation was going on. She got up and went over to the window where she pulled back the curtain and looked out.

Two men appeared to be having a slow-motion wrestling match on the pavement outside. Each held the other's arms as they swayed this way and that. She quickly put on her dressing-gown and went downstairs. A glance at her bedside clock showed that it was just after eleven. Switching on the porch light, she cautiously opened the front door. One of the men disengaged himself and ran off while the other looked uncertainly in her direction. She recognised him as the burly young man with

173

a beard she had seen in the shelter.

'What's going on?' she called out in a tone that surprised her by its imperious note.

He hesitated a second, then reluctantly opened the front gate and advanced towards her.

'Sorry you've been disturbed, lady,' he said. 'It was a drunk, but he's scarpered now. It won't happen again.'

'Who exactly are you?' Sarah asked in the same tone.

The young man frowned and scratched his head.

'Not supposed to answer that,' he said awkwardly. 'Not doing anyone any harm, anyway.'

'If you don't tell me exactly what you're up to out there, I'll call the police. And the fire brigade and anyone else I can think of.'

'No need for that,' he said gruffly. After a pause in which he had a further scratch of his head, he added, 'We're monitoring a cable that runs outside.'

'What sort of cable?'

'Just a cable.'

'I don't believe you. I think you're bugging my telephone.'

He threw her a look of genuine surprise. 'We wouldn't need to pitch camp outside your house to do that, lady,' he said with a note of relief.

'Well, I'm going to make an official complaint first thing in the morning, so you'd better either pack up and leave or get ready to answer someone else's questions.'

She closed the front door firmly and immediately switched off the porch light to show him who held the initiative. She had been surprised by her boldness, but was far from thinking she had won any sort of victory.

She went into the kitchen and made herself another hot drink. She knew that sleep was out of the question.

There wasn't the slightest doubt in her mind that the man on the pavement who had run off was Peter.

174

Chapter 24

Three days later eight people gathered in the Attorney-General's room in the Law Officers Department in London. Apart from the A-G and his senior permanent official, there were high-ranking representatives of MI5 and MI6, the Director of Public Prosecutions and various minions, though this would not have been their own choice of description. Amongst them was Geoffrey Traill.

'So what's the urgency? Why have we had to get together at such short notice?' the A-G asked, surveying the faces on the other side of his desk.

'The case has now been committed for trial,' the man from MI5 said.

'I'm aware of that, but it won't be listed for weeks and we could probably get it kept out for even longer if we wanted.'

'The trouble is that Atkins is becoming dangerously restive,' the man from MI5 said, glancing towards Geoffrey Traill.

Traill nodded vigorously. 'That's almost an understatement,' he said. 'Three nights ago he managed to give us the slip and tried to visit his wife. There was an awkward scene on the pavement outside the house involving one of our men and Mrs Atkins came out to see what was happening. I'm not exaggerating when I say that Atkins is in an extremely volatile state at the moment. He could do something unpredictable.'

The A-G was thoughtful for a while. 'Is it really out of the question that he should give evidence if the defence want to call him?'

Geoffrey Traill looked alarmed. 'He'd be as good as signing his death warrant if he appeared. He'd be bound to have his photograph taken and that would be the beginning of the end.'

175

'He's in as much danger as that?'

'Yes.'

The MI5 and MI6 men added their own nods of agreement and Geoffrey Traill wiped his brow.

'We're pretty sure they're already on to him,' he went on. 'A bogus insurance salesman called on Mrs Atkins about a week ago and looked around for photographs of her husband in the house. Fortunately there weren't any, but it was then that we decided to remove him to a place of safety.'

'Does Mrs Atkins have no idea of his background?' the A-G enquired.

'None. Though she's certainly become suspicious in recent weeks.'

'And what sort of a marriage has it been?'

'Highly successful until all this happened,' Traill said ruefully. 'If only she had run over a nonentity instead of a public figure.'

'It might have been even better if she hadn't run over anyone at all,' the A-G observed drily. He looked towards the D.P.P. 'What's the actual strength of the case against Mrs Atkins?'

'It all turns on the evidence of one witness, the girl Cheryl Peterson.'

'I gather she was severely cross-examined in the magistrates' court, but survived.'

'Yes and no, Attorney. She didn't break down and admit to perjury; on the other hand she departed from her original statement in such a way as to indicate a certain lack of regard for the truth. In fact she admitted as much.'

'Have you spoken to Robert Gidman since the case?'

'Yes, I went to see him yesterday and we had a long talk.'

'Does he believe the witness is telling the truth on the vital issue of the car lights?'

'He said that if he were on the jury, he'd find it difficult to accept her evidence without corroboration.'

'And is there any?'

'None. It's word against word.'

'And Mrs Atkins hasn't yet given evidence on oath?'

'No.'

'I understand that her husband initially supported his wife's version of events, but subsequently back-tracked.' He cast an enquiring look at Geoffrey Traill.

'I can explain that,' Traill said with a slight squirm. 'After I'd told him it was out of the question for him to appear anywhere near the court and run the risk of being photographed, he went to see Miss Epton and was driven into saying that he couldn't give evidence anyway because he'd been asleep in the car when the accident happened.'

'I don't imagine she accepted that very happily.'

'No.'

'No more would I!' He turned back to the D.P.P. 'Has Robert Gidman any theory as to why this witness should be lying?'

'He thinks she probably switched on the lights to protect her boyfriend – it would have been before she knew he'd been mortally injured – and was then stuck with the lie. She's only eighteen and has a domineering father who's something of a barrack-room lawyer from all accounts. She was left to cope with a situation in the only way she knew how.'

The A-G pursed his lips. 'On the face of it, of course, Mrs Atkins had much more reason to lie than Miss Peterson. Defendants always have.'

The D.P.P. nodded. 'With that in mind I also had a word with Sergeant Hibbert, the officer who interviewed both women after the accident. I gather he's a very level-headed sort of person and he certainly sounded such when I spoke to him. He said that though he was aware defendants lied to get themselves out of trouble, he'd been impressed by Mrs Atkins and, if it came to a simple choice, he'd prefer her word to Miss Peterson's.'

'And as we all know, it's not just a simple choice between the one and the other,' the A-G remarked. 'The burden of proof rests on the prosecution.' He turned his gaze on the senior MI5 representative. 'I know it's not strictly relevant to what we're considering, but explain to me how Mr Jablonski fits into the overall picture.'

'He was a Polish exile who had been in this country since the end of the war and who did a number of jobs for us. We used his

177

address on a number of occasions, one of them being when we were fitting Atkins up with references for his job in Worthing. Later, Jablonski's marriage began to break up and he took to the bottle and became generally unreliable so that we decided not to use him any more. Also about that time we became suspicious that he was double-crossing us. Nothing was ever proved, though our suspicions remained. When his marriage finally collapsed, he went off to live in Canada.

'Would he have known who Atkins was?' the A-G broke in.

'He could have done,' the MI5 man remarked unhappily. 'We're still trying to find out what brought him back to this country, but his return confirms our suspicions that he may have become a double. It's clear he was tortured before being killed and he may have opened his mouth wide in order to try and save his life. He should, of course, have known better; it merely precipitated his death.'

'It's a chilling sort of world you operate in,' the A-G observed with a faint smile. He glanced round the assembled faces. 'So, what are we going to do?'

'Time is definitely not on our side,' Geoffrey Traill broke in anxiously. 'An immediate decision is vital.'

The A-G frowned his annoyance at the intervention. Glancing at the D.P.P. he said, 'What would you have me do, Director?'

'If one accepts everything we've been told about the danger to Atkins, there's only one answer, a *nolle prosequi*. That would put an end to the court proceedings and nobody could question your decision.'

'Nobody? I can think of a number of my parliamentary colleagues, who not only could, but would. They'd want to know the reason behind it. I'm aware that my authority to enter a *nolle prosequi* can't be questioned by the courts, but, for those of you who don't know the niceties, it's usual to direct it to be entered only in cases where an accused person cannot be produced in court owing to physical or mental incapacity which has overcome them and which is likely to be permanent. That's certainly not Mrs Atkins's position.'

'I agree,' the D.P.P. said, 'that you'd be entering it in unusual

178

circumstances.'

'So what reason would I give?'

'If you agree in principle, Attorney, perhaps we could discuss later how to wrap it up in a form palatable to the public.'

'I doubt whether any amount of wrapping up is going to be palatable to Jonathan Cool's family and fans,' the A-G observed gloomily. 'Incidentally, there's one legal requirement we've not mentioned. I can't enter a *nolle* until the bill of indictment has been signed.'

'I'm sure that can be organised within a couple of days,' the D.P.P. said. 'I'll speak to the court administrator myself and explain the situation. I'm certain there won't be any difficulty.'

The A-G turned the pages of the file in front of him with an abstracted air. 'And you really believe this man's life will be in danger if his wife's trial goes ahead and he appears as a witness?'

'There's no doubt about it in our minds,' the senior MI5 man said.

'Wouldn't it still be possible to have a trial without his evidence?'

'Miss Epton would certainly be shouting on the court roof if that were suggested.'

'Not if you took her into your confidence.'

'A *nolle prosequi* would be much simpler,' the MI5 man said.

'For you, perhaps! You won't have to face the public furore.' The A-G stared out of the window as if he could already see the blade of the guillotine glinting in the sunlight. When he turned back, he said in a suddenly brisk tone, 'I confess I have less hesitation than I would have had in view of what I've been told about the quality of Miss Peterson's evidence.'

'So you agree to a *nolle prosequi*, Attorney?' the D.P.P. said with an air of relief.

'I don't seem to have much choice. Perhaps you'd now care to advise me how to sell my decision to the public. . . .'

179

Chapter 25

'Guess what's happened!' Rosa said when she burst into her partner's room a few days later, her eyes bright with excitement. 'I've just had a call from the D.P.P. himself to say that the Attorney-General is entering a *nolle prosequi* in the Atkins case.'

Robin Snaith blinked in surprise. 'Did he tell you why?'

'He merely said there was a security aspect involved, but that he wasn't at liberty to say more. He asked me not to tell anyone apart from my client. He also said the breathalyser charge would be dropped.'

'The decision presumably relates to Peter Atkins's position and means we can now rule out some of our more fanciful theories. He'll hardly be a convicted murderer on release from prison; nor a sleeper, unless the powers-that-be are even more devious than one imagines. And if he's one of our own intelligence operatives, what on earth was he doing teaching English at Mr Jameson's? I agree it would be a good cover, but cover for what?'

'I have a theory,' Rosa said.

'Another? What is it this time?'

She gave him a sly smile. 'I'll write it down and put the piece of paper in a sealed envelope which you can keep in your safe until all is revealed. Then you can open it and see if I was right.'

'What guarantee is there that all will ever be revealed? There've been enough efforts to conceal the truth so far.'

'One day something is bound to come out,' Rosa said as she turned to go back to her own room. 'I must phone Sarah and give her the glad news.'

'Hello, Stan, haven't seen you in our court for a while.' The speaker was one of the clerks in the office at Chichester Crown Court.

'My last three cases have all gone to Lewes,' Stan said with his customary air of self-importance, referring to the fact that Lewes Crown Court at the other end of the county was designated a first tier court and was empowered to try the more serious crimes in the country. 'I was a bit surprised the justices sent the Cool case to your court,' he went on. 'I know you're competent to deal with it and all that, but it ought to be tried by a High Court judge at Lewes.'

His companion gave him a small superior smile. 'For once you're not up to date, Stan.' He lowered his voice. 'For your ears only, it's not going to be tried anywhere.'

'What d'you mean?'

'Can't say more at the moment, but you'll know soon enough.' He frowned. 'Anyway, your firm's not involved in that case, is it?'

'No, but I have a considerable interest in it. My daughter's the chief witness for the prosecution.'

'Of course, I was forgetting. She was Cool's girlfriend in the car, wasn't she? Got over the shock of it, has she?' He glanced about him to make sure they couldn't be overheard. 'Keep this under your hat, but the Attorney-General's entering a *nolle prosequi.*'

'What are you on about?' Stan asked in a mixture of disbelief and outrage.

'Keep your voice down! I shouldn't be telling you as it's not yet public knowledge, but that's the position. No trial.'

'You must be joking!'

'No, I'm not, it's a fact,' his companion said, beginning to wish he had never spoken. 'I only told you for your daughter's sake.'

'But why's he doing this?' Stan asked in a furious voice.

'Don't ask me! The Attorney-General doesn't have to give the court any explanation for his decision.'

By the time Stan Peterson reached home his mood was one of burning anger and indignation. His wife saw it written all over his face the moment he entered the house.

'Where's Cheryl?' he asked.

'She's gone to a film with Debbie. Why, what's happened?'

181

As he told his wife what he'd heard, he failed to notice the expression of profound relief that came over her face.

'I'm certainly not going to let the matter rest there,' he went on furiously. 'The Attorney-General's a Minister of the Crown and answerable to the public for his actions. I intend finding out what's been going on behind the scenes. It's absolutely disgraceful.'

'Don't you think it's more up to Jonathan's family to ask questions if they want? It's not really our business.'

'I'm certainly making it my business. I'm a free citizen of this country *and* a taxpayer and I've every right to know. Anyway, I owe it to Cheryl.'

'I don't think you'll find Cheryl will want to quarrel with the Attorney-General's decision,' his wife said quietly. 'Frankly, she's had enough, Stan. I see more of her than you do and I know she's close to a breakdown. I very much doubt whether she'd have been fit to give evidence again. It could scar her mind for life. As a matter of fact I was proposing to go and talk to the doctor and arrange for her to see a psychiatrist.'

'You've never mentioned any of this to me,' he remarked huffily.

'It doesn't alter the fact that it's what I had in mind. I was going to tell you later.' She came over to where he was sitting and took one of his hands in hers. 'Sometimes, Stan, things do work out for the best and I believe this is one of them. I don't often give you advice, but take it from me that it wouldn't be in Cheryl's interests to go through the ordeal of a further court appearance. It could really unbalance her mind and that's the last thing either of us would wish.' She rested a hand on his forehead. 'Slip off your shoes and I'll make us a pot of tea. We can have a nice quiet evening at home together.'

Out in the kitchen, she blinked away the tears that suddenly began to trickle down her cheeks. Her sense of relief was unbounded and the Attorney-General, of whom she had scarcely ever been aware, still seemed a most unlikely saviour.

182

Epilogue

'Mrs Sayers? I'm Claudia Bishop. I'm chairman of the Good
Neighbours Association.' She grinned, exposing long front teeth
and a good deal of gum. 'I meant chairman, too; I've no patience
with all this chairperson nonsense.' The grin became a horsey
chortle. 'I'm afraid I was away when you arrived or I'd have
called sooner. Anyway, is there anything I can do? You're settling
in all right, I hope. I think you'll find us a friendly community; on
the other hand we don't intrude into one another's lives. You're
from London, I gather?'

'Yes.'

Mrs Bishop peered into the hall. 'Is that your daughter? What
a pretty child, how old is she?'

'Nearly two-and-a-half.'

'A lovely age. Well, I expect you're busy, so I won't keep you
talking on the doorstep. I'll give you my card and then you can
phone me if you need any help or advice. You'll find Devon very
different from London.'

'I expect so.'

'Is your husband working locally?'

'He's with Brigstock Publications.'

'Splendid! Such a good firm and I know Mr Brigstock has
never regretted the day he moved his business out of London. We
were all a bit anxious at first that his plant might prove to be
something of an eyesore, but they've done a splendid bit of
landscaping. Is your husband on the printing or publishing side?'

'The publishing.'

'Splendid. Well, I really must be off. It's been so nice meeting

183

you, Mrs Sayers. Incidentally, please call me Claudia.' The invitation was unmistakable.

'I'm Sarah.'

'Well, goodbye, Sarah – it's one of my favourite names. I'll be in touch with you again soon. Perhaps you and your husband would care to come round for drinks and meet a few of the locals?'

'My husband's not been very well recently, so perhaps. . .'

'No need to say anything more, I quite understand. But, meanwhile, don't hesitate to call on my services if I can help over anything. I have the reputation for knowing the answers to most things.' With a brisk wave of a gloved hand she turned and set off at a trot towards her car parked along the road.

Sarah closed the front door and returned to the kitchen to find that Nicole had managed to cover herself with flour. She wiped her daughter's hands and face and set her at the table to draw her favourite animals.

It still seemed to her that she had been Sarah Atkins of Worthing one day and Sarah Sayers in a house outside Exeter the next. Everything had happened with such incredible suddenness. Nicole and Peter were the only realities that remained in her life. And Peter was no longer the same person. In the first place he was now Robert Sayers, though Sarah flatly refused to call him anything other than Peter. As a result Geoffrey Traill had felt obliged to provide her with an explanation for calling him Peter when everyone else would know him as Robert. Traill and others had been clinically thorough in arranging the metamorphosis. A fresh home, together with passports, driving licences and everything else that could be thought of, had been supplied to fit their new identities. Money had apparently been no object.

The worst part had been the severance of all previous ties and Sarah recalled with distress an awkward goodbye to a puzzled Mr Jameson.

Throughout the drama, Peter had been tender and loving, though Sarah frequently found herself giving him sidelong looks. It wasn't merely that his physical appearance had altered, for he now wore a beard, but he was no longer the person she had

184

married. He was no longer Peter Atkins with an obscure background he preferred not to talk about. And yet despite everything she knew she was still deeply in love with him.

To him the change from Peter Atkins to Robert Sayers had merely been another move in a dangerous game, for the one name was as much an attached label as the other.

It was five years since Nikolai Antonov, a senior K.G.B. officer in the Soviet Embassy in Bonn had defected to the West, bringing with him the sort of information that caused its intelligence services to feel that some benign deity must after all be on their side.

After a lengthy debriefing he had emerged into the world as Peter Atkins, aware that he would be a hunted man for the rest of his days, for intelligence services, least of all the K.G.B., never forgive those who betray their secrets.

And everything had been all right until that misty October evening when Sarah had had the misfortune to run down Jonathan Cool, an accident that threw their lives into jeopardy.

She now believed that knowledge of his true background had helped her survive the crisis, for there were no longer any barriers between them. He had told her that he had a divorced wife in Moscow, but no children. He had wept when he spoke of his aged parents living in Kiev and Sarah had wept with him. He had described his upbringing and how he had perfected his English and German so that he could pass as a native of either country. He told her how he had been recruited into the K.G.B. and how eventually he had become totally disenchanted with the system under which he had grown up and had determined to defect. He told her many other things as well, including what he had been doing on Worthing railway station when he was seen by Cecily Young. He had been on the way to a hastily arranged meeting with Geoffrey Traill in the anonymity of Brighton, but had been obliged to take a later train after she had spotted him on the same platform.

'With your help, my darling, I shall be all right,' he had said the previous evening. 'Cats have nine lives and ex-K.G.B. officers

185

have as many.' He had refrained from adding that they needed them, too.

They had made love and for the first time in weeks Sarah had felt the tension go out of her.

It had been the security service psychiatrist, with whom she had had a lengthy interview, who had suggested she should consider having another baby as part of the therapy of adjustment. She had been in no frame of mind to accept the suggestion then, but had since given the idea increasing thought. She also knew how eager Peter was to have a son.

'I see that the Attorney-General answered a parliamentary question about the Atkins case yesterday,' Robin remarked to Rosa about a week later. 'It was as bland and unforthcoming as one might have expected. He merely said it wouldn't be in the public interest to give reasons for his decision to enter a *nolle prosequi* and he flatly refused to budge from that.'

Rosa nodded. 'I imagine he'd found out that he could get away with saying a polite nothing. Incidentally, I'd not heard anything from Sarah since I phoned her the news, but I had a note this morning.' She went on with a slightly puzzled air. 'It had a London postmark, but bore no address other than a box number. She said they'd left Worthing and that she'd get in touch with me as soon as they were settled. Otherwise it was just to thank me for all I'd done.'

'Presumably the box number is one operated by our faceless friends.'

'I'd think so. It rather confirms my theory about her husband.'

'It's obviously time to open that envelope.'

Without waiting for a reply, Robin got up and went across to his wall safe.

'You open it,' Rosa said, when he handed the envelope to her.

Robin did so and read out, 'By a process of elimination I now conclude the P.A. is an Eastern Bloc defector, possibly from the K.G.B. or suchlike.' He looked up and met Rosa's gaze. 'If you're right,' he said, 'we'll certainly never be told.' He took out his lighter and, after a nod from Rosa, set fire to the piece of paper in his hand.

'I just hope they manage to rebuild their lives,' Rosa remarked. 'I'm sure Sarah has all it needs and Peter, too, if he's what I think.'